AGATHA *and* FRANK'S STORY

AGATHA *and* FRANK'S STORY

Stranded on Rosland Island

JOLYNN ROSE

ARPress
45 Dan Road Suite 5
Canton MA 02021

Hotline: 1(888) 821-0229
Fax: 1(508) 545-7580

Ordering Information:
Quantity sales. Special discounts are available on quantity purchases by corporations, associations, and others. For details, contact the publisher at the address above.

Printed in the United States of America.

ISBN-13:   Softcover   979-8-89389-152-2
              eBook   979-8-89389-151-5

Library of Congress Control Number: 2024914334

ACKNOWLEDGEMENTS

Thanks again to my wonderful Mom, Lola Smith.
These books would have never happened without her!
She not only helped with writing the books, editing,
but she did some of the art work too!

PROLOGUE

FTER MEETING AGGIE (Agatha) at the senior home, we became great friends in a short amount of time. She would tell me stories about when Frank and she were stranded on an island, in 1955 and they lived with the Roslanders, who were Merbeing. As she got closer to death, she asked me to publish her journals about their life's and adventure with the Roslanders and the discovery they found on the island.

Aggies's daughters and daughter-in-law and I have been working on Aggie (Agatha) journals together. The first book we published, Tales of the Merbeing, was cut out of Aggies's journals. We really didn't know how people would take to the book, so we just did a short story. We (Frank and Aggie children; Frank Jr., Twila, Maria and I) all wanted to get the story out about the Merbeings. It was important to let people know that there are other being on this plant.

There are so many people that believe in Merbeing (Mermaids), and had enjoyed reading our first book, Roslander, Tales of the Merbeing Clans. But one question that I keep getting asked "What did Agatha and Frank do while they were stranded on Rosland Island. What did they do when the Roslanders left on their migration?"

It was decided by the family, that we would publish her journals, in the order she had written them. It includes some of the stories from the other books we have already published. But this one is about all the adventure and discoveries Agatha and Frank had discovered on the island. The Rosland Island was once a mountain range connected to a main land, and as time passed the mountain range sank into the ocean. Only the island was left, where once a land mass used to be. The island has two mountains on it, one at each end. There are many stories to tell about Agatha and Frank adventures, and about who used to live on the land mass, beside the Merbeings. This is important to know, because of everything they found.

Here is Agatha journals, in her own words, enjoy!

Jill

Frank and Agatha

CHAPTER

1

I T IS HARD to believe, we are finally going to sail around the islands and live in our sailboat for the next two years. I've started this journal, I want to keep track of everything we see and do. I don't want to forget anything. This has been a dream of Frank and mine, for most our married life. We have traveled a lot, due to Frank career in the Army. It was wonderful, we saw so many wonderful things, and our children learned a lot about the history of our planet. It doesn't hurt having a mom for a history teacher. We lived in Germany for awhile, so we traveled all around Europe.

Frank had just retired from the Army, and I have been retired from being a history teacher for about a year now. Our plan was to travel around the islands in the South Pacific, before we got too old. We were both in our 50s and still in great shape. Our children really weren't too happy about us taken this adventure, but they couldn't stop us. Our plan was to travel from island to island for about two years. We told the kids that we would call them every so often to let them know that we are okay.

Anyway it was a wonderful day, the weather couldn't have been any better. We had been out for a couple of days, we had been island hopping and saw all kinds of sea life on and off the island, and the water was so calm and beautiful. We have done this many times, but this time it felt different, because we would not be going home for two years. We felt so free!

After everyone said their good-byes, we headed out to our first island, St. John Island. The plan is to go up the coast line and then just go where ever the wind blows us. Knowing Frank there will be a lot of planning around that.

We decided to go more east because the weather was starting to look bad. I wanted to go back to the last island we were on, but Frank said "We could out run the storm." Guess who was right! As we turned east the wind picked up, and we were really flying, the boat was going back and forth, flying through the air and when we landed on the water everything went dark for me. I guess I was knocked out. Frank told me "The mainsail hit me in the back and knocked me off my feet." The next thing I know the boat was going every which way again. As the wind was blowing us all around, we hung on for our lives. Frank yelled "The boat is going to hit the rocks, hang on." As the storm continued to push us, then we hit the rocks with a force, and the boat flew into the air and crashed on to the rocks. Then all of sudden the storm disappeared as fast as it had started, it was like the storm was determined to destroy us. But the boat was hung up on a pile of rocks; it was more like a miniature island.

As the weather cleared we could see a bigger island in the distance. We decided that we needed to make our way to that island. Frank started pulling the dinghy into the water, getting it ready to be loaded up with our supplies. Well as much as we could fit into the dinghy. We didn't know how long the boat would stay afloat, we took as much of the supplies as we could.

We headed for the island, as we paddled we discovered that it was farther than we thought. After hours of paddling and spending the night fighting the storm we were exhausted. But we continued to paddle, and we didn't think we'd ever get there.

We started seeing things so we thought; because we were really exhausted. Frank told me to look over there, "Do you see it, there is someone out in the water," he asked again "Do you see it?" I didn't see anything at first but then I saw a person and we started yelling at them. We couldn't understand why anyone would be out that far, but we didn't care. We didn't care why they were out there we were hoping we would be rescued. There was no response from the person, we thought we were just imagining things, because they did not reply and they disappeared.

Then something started hitting the bottom of the dinghy, it was really weird, because it seem like it was helping us move closer to the island. As it continues to bump our dinghy, we tried to look under the dinghy to see what was doing it. We couldn't see anything! We were afraid that it was sharks hitting the dinghy, but as long as they continued to move us towards the island we were happy.

We finally made it to the shore, we got off the dinghy and once we hit the beach we collapsed to the ground, we were so happy to be on land. We tried to get our land legs back. As we sat on the beach I looked at Frank and asked what the hell happened, what are we going to do? Frank just looked at me and said "We'll figure it out, we will be okay."

The first thing we did is pull the dinghy out of the water and started emptying the little bit of supplies we had loaded into the dinghy. Frank went to get wood and look around a little bit to see if there was any type of life. He told me to do an inventory of what we had so we knew what we would need to survive.

After I did the inventory and Frank got back from his walk we both decided to walk in different directions for 20 minute and see if we could find anything or anyone. There wasn't much to find, then it hit me I couldn't believe that we were stranded on an island; I just sat down and started to cry. Frank sat down next to me and patted me on the back and said "We will be okay and were here together and that's all that counts, and were safe."

With Frank being retired army, he took action! I just sat there wondering what to do, looking out at our boat on the rocks, it was so far away. The next thing I hear is Frank yelling to get up and help him. After spending 30 years with this man, I knew I couldn't have been with a better person. It's funny the first thing that came to my mind was, if you were stranded on a deserted island, who would you want to be with? **Now I know**!

The first day we worked on getting our shelter up, we decide to build it by the tree line. Once we had the shelter built, we moved our supplies to the shelter. We did find a stream of fresh water, coming out of the woods; we set up our shelter there. We weren't sure how long the water would last, so we always kept our eyes out for more fresh water. Frank was upset that I wanted to bring my paper and pens with us, along with all of the other supplies; I told him I was going to write about our adventures no matter what. I guess it's the historian in me!

We had spent a lot of the day just looking around trying to find some kind of life and water for ourselves. We had no clue how long we would be here or what will happen to us. After searching part of the island we found bananas and coconuts, and other fruits. We didn't what to get to far from our boat, just in case someone comes by. We weren't sure what the other fruit was but Frank said "What the hell, it's better than nothing". We also had our fishing poles; we figured we had food for now. As the first day came to a close on the island, all I could wonder was what is going to happen to us? How are we going to survive? Will they ever find us? As I floated off to sleep.

It was funny how fast the night went, we were looking up at the stars and we could hear something off in the distance, we couldn't figure out what it was. It sounded like whale calls, but not really, we had heard sounds on the ocean during our travels but nothing like that.

 **2** 

THE NEXT COUPLE of weeks we were exploring the island; we piled wood up for a rescue fire, just in case we saw a ship. We had no clue where we were at, because of the storm blew us all over the ocean. Well it felt like it anyway. We explored some of the island; we didn't want to get too far away from our camp. It seemed like no one has ever been here. One of the things we did every day is search the beach for any new debris that we could use and the other junk we would pile up, either to burn our strip for later use. One of my tasks was to mark the tree, for every day that we have been here. When we started on the third tree we decided it was time to check out more of the island. It didn't look like we were going to be rescued anytime soon. We haven't seen a ship or a plane the whole time we have been stranded here. So we knew we weren't too close to any civilization.

We figured we would be out overnight so we packed some food and supplies for the trip. The island was bigger than we thought, as we walked around the bend all you could see was more beaches, it just kept going. We looked out to sea and saw a storm coming in; we headed to the tree line for safety. Frank and I found a good place to hang our tarp, and set up the camp for the night. We had the tarp hanging down on the beach side to protect us from the wind coming from the ocean. We took some branches from the trees and made our bed. Frank and I were in good shape when we first started our adventure, but now we were even in better shape. Frank had decided to grow a beard and let his hair grow long, and now he is a tall drink of water! I let my hair grow long too and lost the weight that I wanted to before we left on our trip; I don't think I'm looking too bad either, at 5 ft. 8. I also think I'm a tall drink of water, even if I say so myself.

The storm was bigger than the one that had landed us here. So as we sat under cover watching the storm come in, we were glad we had brought the tarp with us, and other supplies. We didn't get much sleep that night, the wind and rain was hard and strong, it was a driving rain, it lasted all night long. In the morning the sun was out and another beautiful day at the beach. At least being stranded on this island most of the time it was beautiful here.

As we look down on the beach, there was all kinds of debris; we thought we hit the jackpot, since there was so much debris everywhere, we were hoping that it was stuff that we could use. As we started looking and picking up things, we notice that things looked familiar. Then Frank yelled, "This is our boat, look at this!" It was a piece of the boat, which had our boat's name on it, BIG DREAM. My heart just dropped, as he held up the wood, then we looked over towards the rock that had held our boat all these weeks, and it was gone.

We started looking through the debris to see what came ashore from our boat. As we were walking along, I saw something move. I yelled at Frank, and pointed at the pile of seaweeds and netting that was in front of me. I told him I saw something moving. So he picked up a piece of wood for an club and we walked towards it, thinking it may be a seal, turtle or some other sea creature that had gotten tied up in the seaweed. When we heard it making a weird noise, it stopped us in our tracks.

Whatever it was it started moving and making more noises. It sounded like it was hurt or scared. We walked slowly up to the pile and that's when we saw it, it looked like a human face, a face of a boy. As we looked at the pile we didn't see any other part of him, but it looked like a fish had tried to eat him because there was a fish tail at the end of the pile. It screamed again and we jump back, you could tell it was scared so Frank handed me the club and said "Stay back, and keep an eye on It," as he reached down the thing started screaming and tried to get away. But it was all tangled up in the seaweed and netting. Frank started talking to it, and it started settling down like it understood what he was saying. As Frank walked over to it, he pulled out his knife and then it started getting upset again, but Frank just kept talking to it. Frank started cutting the seaweed and netting away, as he was cutting it away, we could see it wasn't a fish, it was part of the boy in the seaweed. To our shock it was a mermaid, the upper part looked like a teenage boy. So I guess it was a merboy!

As Frank cuts the merboy loose he started flipping his tail trying to get away, back into the water. But the boy was too far up on the beach. Frank told him that he could help him, by taken my arms and showing him what he wanted to do. Frank put his arms under my arm pit, and pulled me backward. The boy seems to understand us, he shook his head like he had acknowledged us and it was okay to do. Frank was a little scared, but he did it anyway. Frank dragged the boy to the water edge. Once the boy was in the water he took off, then we saw him about 25 feet out in the water. Then we heard the same sound we heard the first night and many nights since, we've been on the island.

After we set the boy free, we just looked at each other. Frank asked me "Was that what I think it was?" I said, what did you think it was? He said "A mermaid", I think so too, but it was a male mermaid, it didn't have any tits, it looked like a young boy to me, but with a tail. He didn't have any hair on his head either." I told Frank, he looked so scared, but he acted like he understood what you were saying to him.

As we looked out to the sea wondering what the hell just happened, we just shook our heads and started picking up the things we wanted to keep for our debris pile for the day. We kept looking at each other wondering did that really happen, were we going crazy being stranded on this island for all this time. Frank said "No, it couldn't be that because we both saw it at the same time and he had touched the boy so he knows it was real." He could always read my mind; I guess that is what happens when you have been married as long as we have. In the next week's we did our cleanup on the beach, every time we saw a pile of seaweed, we hope maybe it was another mermaid. I think mostly to confirm what happened earlier.

I started a journal when we first started our adventure I didn't think I would have so much to write about here on this island. It's a good thing I planned on a long trip. We still hear the strange sounds at night; we think it is the mermaids talking to each other. Every once in a while we think we see the young boy watching us. We wave at him, but he doesn't wave back and dives quickly back into the sea.

 **3** 

I T HAS NOW been six months and there have been no signs of a boat, ship or even a plane. We feel like we are all alone in the world. Frank and I decided it was time to explore the island some more. We tried to stay close to where the boat had crashed, but now it is gone. There really isn't any point in staying here. Frank hung the boat's name on a tree, and added Frank and Agatha were here! Just in case someone finds the island and is looking for us.

We packed up as much as we could and Frank made a storage area, which was a big hole, covered with tree branches and logs, he did this to keep what we left behind safe and protected from the weather, just in case we came back. Until we know how big the island is and what else is on it, we need to keep our options open. It's the military way; always have a plan, A, B, or C. You never know what will happen or what you will need.

As we moved down the beach we felt like someone was watching us. But we didn't see anything on land or in the sea. It felt like we walked for days, because we were carrying so many supplies, but it has only been six hours. Our plan was to walk around the island, and to draw a map of the island as we went.

This way we would know what we had to work with. As we walked we saw turtles sunbathing on the beach. There were also seals, lizards and funny sounds coming from the trees. We may have been the only humans, but the animal life was doing great, we set up camp as the sun set. As much as I love turtles, I love them more at the end of the day, we had turtle soup; it was nice to have a big bowl to work with again. Bless the turtle's!

The next morning when we got up we saw something by the water, so we walked to the water edge, there was two fish just laying there, it had sea plants around it; they were ready to eat. Yes, eating raw fish was part of our diet now. We looked out to the sea and saw the boy waving at us; he must have left the fish for us. Then he disappeared into the water again.

As we ate the fish, we wonder why he did it; we guessed it was his way of thanking us. After breakfast we packed up the camp and headed down the beach. As we walked we wondered what will happen next, and is there any more mermaid people out there. I asked Frank, do you think they can understand us, or does he think we will ever see any more like him.

We finally found the end of the island. There was no beach, there was a high cliff and there was no way around it, except to go into the forest. We hadn't been too far inside the island yet, but it was the only way to find the other side of the island. It looked like it was going to be quite a climb, so we figured it would be better to stay the night on the beach and head out first thing in the morning.

The evenings are wonderful, if I had to guess I would say it would be 70 degrees every night, with a nice little breeze and only the sound of the ocean and the creatures that live here. Inside the island we could hear different sounds, but we really didn't know what they were at this time. We always had a fire because it was more for comfort, than heat. I would have never dreamed this is how we would spend our last years of our lives together.

As we fell asleep we heard the strange sounds again and it almost sounded like people talking. The wind and the forest were playing tricks on us, so we thought! In the morning we headed into the woods, it wasn't too bad, we didn't see any snakes. Maybe, because we're on an island, go figure! As we walked our way through the woods we tried to stay as close to the mountain as we could, we didn't want to make the trip any longer than necessary. After a while we started hearing sounds coming from the mountain. We were trying to decide if we wanted to check it out or not. Frank said, "What the heck, let's go check it out." As we moved closer we could see a small opening to a cave. I asked Frank, do you think there are people living in the cave. I said, let's play it safe and leave our gear here. We will be as quiet as a mouse, as we go up the mountain.

As we got closer to the cave opening, the sound became louder, it sounded weird, and it sounded like people talking with a mix of sea lions all together. The cave would be a great place to camp, but that isn't what happened. The closer we got to the opening it was clear it was people talking in some other language; it wasn't in English of any type or any other language that we have heard before. Frank wanted to go in by himself to make sure it was safe. As we got closer to the cave opening we saw that it opened up inside, big enough for us to walk in. As Frank walked into the cave; I held my breath wondering what he would find. I waited for his signal that it was safe for me to come in. It felt like it took forever, and then I heard it, tap, tap, tap, that was our signal we had agreed on.

I entered the cave, as I got closer to Frank he signaled me to get down. I crawled up next to him, where he was laying on a ledge looking down into a cavern. It was just light enough to see movement; it looked like some kind of sea animal lying on the rocks. As we watched the creatures, we were trying to make out what they were, we assume they were sea lions or maybe some seals, as the Sun started to set, and it lit up the cavern. We could see more creatures coming in to the cave; we couldn't believe what we saw. It was a group of mermaids coming into the cavern. They were making the sounds that we have been hearing from the ocean, but it was more of a musical sound than the one that we normally heard.

All we could do is watch in wonderment, Frank looked at me and I just couldn't say anything. I couldn't believe what we were seeing! As it was getting dark Frank signaled me to move back out of the cavern, as we crawled back out of sight, we stood up and climbed back down the mountain. I turned to Frank and said; I guess were not alone here on the island after all.

While we were setting up the camp at the bottom of the mountain we started talking about what we saw, and what we were going to do next. We agreed to wait until morning when there was more light to see what really was in the cavern. We didn't get much sleep that night, there was another storm, but not as bad as some of them we have seen here. Frank wanted to make contact with the mermaids, but didn't want to upset the group of mermaids. Frank explained to me, that they are not all mermaids we should call them Merbeing. There are male and females in the cavern, and it looks like even families of them. I guess we are Human beings and they are Merbeing.

The next morning we headed back up the mountain, crawled up to the ledge, the cavern was as if the lights have been turned on, and they were all gone. We just looked at each other and wonder what happened to them. We decided to wait and see if they come back, after a few hours we gave up and went back to the camp. That night we went back up to see if they were their again, there was no sign of them. The next morning it was time to move on, to the other side of the island.

As we worked our way through the forest we talked about how we could make contact with these Merbeings. If only they used our language. As we were moving through the forest we noticed that there was wild boars and many different types of birds, one even looked like a chicken. We were wondering how they would taste, eating just fish and sea plants were getting kind of tiring. There were a few different types of trees: bamboo and a few trees I've never seen before. We have tried a few of the different fruit looking things that we found and they weren't too bad, well at least we didn't get sick. We finally made it through the forest, as we came out, it was another clear day, and the water was beautiful. The forest was nice, but we will take the beach life anytime.

We walked out onto the beach, it was different from the other side we were living on, and it had rock formations around it. It was another beach cove, with another cliff, but this time we could walk around it. As we set up camp for the night, we talked about the Merbeing and wonder if we would ever get off this island. We were sure the kids were looking for us; it has been over a year now. Frank went into the forest and killed a chicken, or whatever you want to call the bird, for dinner, and I used some herbs I found in the forest, and of course seaweeds for a soup. We ate a lot of soup these days.

The next day we set off to go around the cliff while the tide was out. As we came around the bend, we could see merbeing lying on the rocks. They just looked at us like we were the strange things, which of course we were thinking they were the strange beings, instead of us. We saw someone waving at us, it was the boy we had saved earlier this year, and we waved back at him. As we walked down to the beach, we started seeing more and more Merbeings. It looks like it is a group of them; they continued to watch as we came closer to them. The smaller merbeings swam away as if they were scared of us. The boy pointed at a rock formation as if to tell us to go over there, to come out to meet him, so we did. The bay looked a lot like a man-made bay; it had a jetty going out to the sea, with an opening in the middle. The rocks were at different levels, they were put in place for a reason. It looks like an ancient city that had thrived at one time with humans as the builders, some of the rocks look like they could have been someone's house at one time. In the middle of the bay there was a tall formation it wasn't just a tall rock it resemble a tower, at one time it could have been in the middle of a town square. It could have been a beautiful city at one time, but some kind of disaster destroyed it.

4

THE BOY SWAM closer to us, and then another Merbeing came up to him and stopped him. It was bigger than the boy, we found out later it was his father, Trido. Merbeing don't look anything like the stories of the sailors that was told to us from the past. They don't have long hair and aren't beautiful, they look like us but they have no hair on their head or face. Their eyes are big and round, a lot like a whale eyes, it feels like they can see right through you. Their nose is a long slit in the face, inside it looks like they have gills that they use for breathing; they have no ears, just holes. We could only see the top part, the arms are long, and their hands are like ours, except their skin in between their fingers. The skin looks like dolphin skin, gray but soft and look light on the belly. The mouth was small to, but they didn't use it to talk to each other. They could talk to each other by reading each other's minds. We found out later that is how they communicate with each other. Trido was much bigger then Tride, his upper body was very muscular looking, whereas Tride was still growing.

The bigger Merbeing said "Hello," which of course, shocked us, we of course said hello back, the Merbeing said "I'm Trido this is my child Tride, and this is our home." His English wasn't very good, but we could understand him, we were surprised that he spoke English at all. Frank introduced himself, my name, as he put his hand on his chest is Frank, and this is my wife Agatha, as he pointed at me, all I could do is wave. Then a female swam up to Trido, and he said "This is Esaw," my wife as he pointed at me. Frank smiled and said "I understand." Esaw had a feminine look about her, and she also had breast so it was obvious she was a female. I think as far as Merbeing go, she was very pretty.

I was thinking to myself what now; we just looked at each other, and wonder what was next. Then Trido put his hand out and indicated us to sit. As we sat down, we really didn't know what was going on or what was going to happen. Esaw spoke to us, thank you for helping our son, he got caught up in the storm, and he shouldn't have been out there. She looked at him as only a parent could do, which made him feel bad. Esaw said, "Normally, we all go to the caverns when there is a bad storm coming in." I told her that we were glad that we could help. Esaw said "That they have been watching us every since the boat hit the rocks. We watched you try to come to shore with the little boat, so we helped you by pushing your boat." Frank said "That was you; we didn't know how come we started moving to the island. Thank you we didn't know if we would have made it otherwise." Esaw said, "We try to help the humans when we can without giving ourselves away, it can be dangerous for us to be seen or caught by humans."

Frank asked about the sounds we have been hearing at night, "Is that from your people?" Trido said "Yes, that is how we signal each other when there is danger or we want them to come in, when we are above the water, otherwise we communicate through the water." Frank didn't know if he wanted to tell them that we have found their cave, but he decided to wait until we got to know them better. As we sat there more Merbeing came to see the weird humans on the rocks. Trido pointed out that this is the first time they have gotten this close to human's before, a few of them acted like they could be in danger.

We felt welcome by these beings, there was only a few of them that didn't come over. Some of them gave us presents, to our amazement it was things from our sailing boat. It was a surprise to see the different items, the pans, glasses and other things they retrieved from it. These were things that we couldn't carry on our dinghy, but would've been nice to have. We are very thankful to them for their gifts. They acted as if they were proud of these items.

We spend many hours trying to learn each other language and the different ways we live. As time went on we have built a little place by the forest and enjoyed learning from the Merbeings on how to swim better (we were both good swimmer, but nothing like the Merbeings). The Merbeing have a city under the water, and there is also a city in the bay. We have found statues, and the tower we had seen earlier was a tower in the middle of a courtyard.

It has been a few weeks since we have arrived at Roslanders city. When we first met our new friends, we really didn't expect to be here this long. They have taken us into their family; we have learned to communicate with them. I love the stories of the past history that the Merbeings have told us. They have been around as long as time has been here. That's how they stated it. Esaw says that her ancestors were here when the monsters roamed the seas. Being a history teacher, I had a lot of questions about their history and wanted to make sure I documented it. Esaw enjoyed telling me all about her people. She started with when their people first started keeping track of their past, pretty much like the humans did. They had written much of their history on the cave walls, that they used to live in, which are no longer under water but on the land.

When the monsters were in the seas, the merbeing stayed close to the coastline. But as the earth changed they had to move across the ocean. It was a dangerous time but they had no choice. They would break up in two groups and swim together to give the impression of being a big fish. This way the monsters would not attack, the hope was that the monster wouldn't attack such a big fish. If the monster did attack the group, then the whole tribe wouldn't be wiped out and the others still would be alive, to continue their line. In time they started to swim with other sea life, this protected them; in return they would help and remove sea urchins from their friend's bodies. From the way, Esaw explain the sea life, I think it was whales, dolphins and turtles.

We talked about many things, I wanted to document their history, even if no human will ever see it, and I felt it was important to write their history down. The next big event they had to live through was when the water moved back, receded from my understanding. At one time they had most of the planet, they lived in the caves and had the open sea to themselves, and then everything changed. The water receded and they lost their homes and cities to the land. Esaw said "At one time, the caves were underwater, the earth moved, caused the water to leave, leaving their home gone, the water had dropped 1000s of feet. They had to move more and more into the ocean. For thousands of years the water moved back, the land was taking over the planet. They had to learn new ways of life and how to deal with the loss of the homes and their way of life."

Esaw and her mother Msaw loved to tell the stories of the Merbeings and all the different things that have happened to not only their clan, but other clans too. Many nights we would sit out at the bay and listen to their stories, with the rest of the Roslanders.

Every day is pretty much the same, we keep hoping to be rescued, but every morning we wake up still on the island. This journal is getting full, so I need to start another one. Who knows what will happen next, Frank and I agreed we need to start doing more exploding on land.

5

I STARTED A NEW journal; Frank and I have been stranded on Rosland Island for a little over a year now. I guess I should note that this is my journal, Agatha Smith (aka Aggie). Frank, my husband and I have been living here, with the Merbeings, who are called the Roslanders and learning all about them. We also have been exploring the island and the water around the island. I decided it was important to note, who we are, in the beginning of my journals just in case we never leave here. If my journals are ever found, at least the person would know who wrote them.

Frank has made an area, where I can store my journals. It protects them from the weather and whatever else that could happen to them. Well as long as the island doesn't sink! Frank made a hole in the ground and then lined the hole with flat stones, which fit so snug that nothing can get through to them. He found the stones in the ancient city, we had discovered earlier this year.

The Roslanders have welcomed us into their clan and we have met other Merbeings from other clans too. The Roslanders are wonderful beings. After we got to know each other a little, we all agreed that it would be a good idea for us to move to Roslanders bay.

The Roslanders went out to our boat which was at the bottom of the ocean and brought pretty much everything they could salvage from it. Frank even joined them to pull the bigger items out of the boat. They would pull him on the raft to where the boat had sunk, where it had hit the rocks. It wasn't that deep so Frank was able to dive with the Roslanders. He showed them how to remove things from the boat, things they normally would not pull out for themselves. They pulled out the water tank, toilet and other things that would be nice to have here on the island, he even brought me a mirror from the cabin of the boat. We have linen, kitchen items, pots, dishes, and silverware. Just like at home!

The boat was pretty well scrapped by the time Frank and the Roslanders were done with it. There wasn't much wood on the boat that we could use to build cabinets to store things. There was lots of wood washing ashore and the island had lots of trees that we could use to build anything else we may need.

Once we settled into the bay area with the Roslanders, every day we would have a project to do, even if it was to clean up the beach. When we cleaned the beach, we would always fined ropes and nets, in with the sea weeds, which had been washed ashore. Many days there wasn't anything to write about, but I still put the date in my journal. This way we could keep track of time, after awhile it was hard to keep track of what day it is.

Every day we hoped to be rescued and someday we would see our children again. We do have pictures of our children on our wall in the house by the forest. The pictures were one of the first things I grabbed and put in our raft when we had to desert our boat.

We have an album of our going away party, and other pictures we knew we would want to look at in our travels. Our plan was to travel around the United States coastal line and head to the Caribbean or wherever else we wanted to go. We never dreamed we would get shipwrecked on an island with Merbeing. I am so glad that I had brought all of the pictures that I did. Every night Frank and I were asking the same question "I wonder what the kids are doing?"

Today was a chicken grabbing day. Frank said he was tired of chasing our food every time we wanted to have chicken; he had a plan to cage the chickens. We finally had enough rope and netting to make a cage. We used the netting and rope that we had found on the beach. We inserted the rope through the holes on top and bottom of the netting. This way we could connect them together. Then we tied the ropes to the trees. We now have a cage. It wasn't the prettiest' thing but hopefully, it will keep the chickens in.

We wouldn't secure the fourth side until we chased the chicken into the cage. Then we would secure the fourth side (netting) trapping the chickens inside. As we were running through the woods yelling and clapping our hands, I turned to watch Frank. It was the funniest thing I've seen in a long time. He had a stick in his hand, and jumping up and down and screaming like a crazy man. The cage was big enough so the chickens would have their normal food supply and lots of room to move around. The cage was small enough so we could catch them, by chasing them into the net. I'm really glad that the Roslanders couldn't see us running around the woods. I'm sure they would have gotten a good laugh out of it.

We hadn't planned to put the pigs into the chicken cage, but they ran into the cage with the chickens, so now we can have pork when we want it too. We try not to treat them like pets, but we both have our favorite pig, his name is Charlie and our favorite chicken name is Angel, she's white and loves to fly. So we will have eggs too!

I also have started a garden. I have transplanted some of the plants that we would eat regularly to the garden. Some of the plants that I wanted were on the other side of the island, that's why I transplanted them to the garden. It is weird how each side of the island has different plants and trees.

I decided to have a garden, because I got so sick earlier this year. I also went to Esaw, the Queen of the Merbeing and my best friend and Koro, the healer of the Roslanders and us. I asked them if they could teach me about the herbs on the island and the ones in the water that surround us. They agreed and acted like they would be happy to do it, I think it was to make sure I didn't eat something I shouldn't again.

Koro would bring plants from the water and I would bring the plants from the land that I wanted to know if we could eat or not. I also wanted to know what plants would be good for healing us, in case we get hurt or sick again.

Koro, the healer had so much information, she had learned everything from her ancestors. She had come from a long line of healer's; she can't remember anyone in her family that hadn't been a healer. They continued to gather their information about the different ways to heal and to find food we could use for eating and cooking.

It took about a week, three to four hours each day, before I had enough information to start my garden. After my classes, I started my garden, it's great to just go out the back door and pick out what type of food I want for dinner. When Frank goes fishing I have him pick up different plants that are in the water. Sometimes he gets a little carried away with picking the plants. So I will use some of it for dinner that night, and the rest I will dehydrate and crush for seasoning later. Nothing goes to waste here.

I learned how to dehydrate and smoke food the old-fashioned way when I was in college. I went to college to be a history teacher, one of the classes I took we spent two weeks living the life of a pioneer. I never thought I would ever use the things I learned, and now this is how we live. We also have a smoker that Frank had built; because we normally couldn't eat all of the food from the pig or the chicken. By smoking the meat, it would last us for a week, if not longer. Sometimes we would even smoke the fish Frank would catch.

We used a lot of the stones that we had found in the ancient city to build our different fire pits and smoker. The rocks are made just right for this type of things, in fact I'm pretty sure that some of them were used for that reason centuries ago. I could tell by the black marks on them, if you use them enough the black is in bedded into the stones.

We are pretty well settled in here, we even put up a little wall around our house, and our little pathway leading to the beach. Well we didn't really make the pathway we found it. It is more of a patio; it is part of the ancient city too.

It seems kind of silly to sweep a dirt floor, but it gives me something to do. But I did notices that the floor was getting harder with time. I would add water to the ground after I would sweep the floor, which helped keep the dust down. I learned this when I went to the pioneer week.

CHAPTER

 **6** 

WE JUST FINISHED our second Batjak with the Merbeings; we had a wonderful time as usual, and got to meet with the other clans that came this year for the event. It was interesting to hear the history of the other clans that live farther away from us. They never really told us exactly where they lived, but it sounded very tropical. All of the Merbeings have been friendly to us, although they all have complained about the human race and the way that they just destroy the waters around them. But humans complain about humans destroying our planet too!

It is hard to believe we have been here so long, I don't know what Frank and I would have done without the Roslanders. We have days that are harder on us than others, such as the children's birthdays and the other events. I hate thinking about all of the things we have missed in the last two years. We wonder what our kids are doing. Our son Frank Jr., was married before we left, and had one boy named Daniel. We also have two daughters Twila and Maria. Twila is married and has a daughter named Tina and Maria is our youngest, she is also married and just had a baby girl before we left, her name is Enola. The reason I'm putting this in my journal is because I miss them all, but also if someone finds my journal they will know who to give them to. All of our kids live in Houston, TX, please give them my journals.

I guess this is one of those days when I am sad that I'm here, instead of with my family. But most of the time, this is such a wonderful place and the beings here treat us so well it is hard not to be happy.

Enough of this, we are planning on going to the other side of the island and exploring the waters there. We had seen a tall stone sticking up out in the bay on that side, so we figured it's time to go do some exploring over there. We normally do this type of thing when the Roslanders have left on their migration, but this time they are still here. Tride and Tridax asked if they could join us in exploring the waters on the other side. How could we say no to them?

When we headed over to the other side of the island we noticed there was a lot of damage to the ancient city in the areas that we had explored earlier. It must've happened during the earthquake that we had. It wasn't that big of an earthquake, but it did knockdown some stones, and we noticed that there were openings and it looked like there was space underneath them.

"We need to go check out those areas where there is now an opening and see what is inside of them. I guess we can do it after the Roslanders leave for their migration, hopefully there will be something interesting for us to find." Frank said.

After climbing over trees and rocks and scaring away the animals, we finally arrived on the other side of the island. Tride and Tridax were already waiting for us. I'm sure it's much easier to swim around the island than it is to go through the woods. Well as long as you don't run into any predators out in the waters!

Before heading out, Frank grabbed the scuba equipment, he had made from different parts we had received from the Roslanders. He had made both of us scuba gear. The Roslanders had found the equipment in different shipwrecks. As we got ready to go into the water, Tridax had already dived down and came up with an old pot. He told us he would show us where he found it; and that there were a lot more of them." One nice thing about having Merbeings helping, they can look around and find things a lot faster than us.

Frank yelled back at him "Were on our way!"

As soon as we reached them, Tride and Tridax disappeared into the water, they couldn't wait to go exploring. As they went under the water, within minutes, we could see them about fifty feet away from us. Tridax was pointing at the location he had found the pots earlier. You could tell he was very anxious for us to see what he had discovered.

We swam towards them; we could see buildings, at least they looked like they could have been buildings at one time. It looked like it must have been part of the city that was located on the island. When we caught up to the guys, Tride pointed out the area where Tridax had found everything. There were all kinds of pots and statues and many other things lying everywhere. Most of the things were in a large room; with something that looked like a fireplace or maybe even a cooking area at one time. Many of the rooms had different statues and lots of sea plants and fish swimming around in them. But at one time it must've been a beautiful city.

7

AFTER EXPLORING THE first area in the city, it was time for us to go to the surface; we were running out of air. We had learned to hold our breath for a long time but we are still human. The underwater breathing tanks that Frank had made for us worked great, but as time has gone on he has continued to make improvements on them. The original one had been made out of whale stomach, but that was gross. The Roslanders had discovered some scuba gear awhile ago so we use the masks now. The Roslanders continue to bring Frank different parts that they would find in the ocean. At one point they even brought back more scuba gear, including the oxygen tanks, but the tanks ran out of air so we couldn't use them anymore. Besides Frank's invention were a lot easier for me to manage than the heavy old tanks.

Trido helped Frank with his inventions, because he liked the idea of us being underwater with them. At the beginning he thought it was funny to see us swimming around with the gear on us. But it was nice for us to be able to see them inside their city. They do spend a lot of time in their city under the water. If we wanted to visit with them we would set up our air tanks and visit them in their Bay City. I asked Frank to draw his air tank invention. It's really neat how it works!

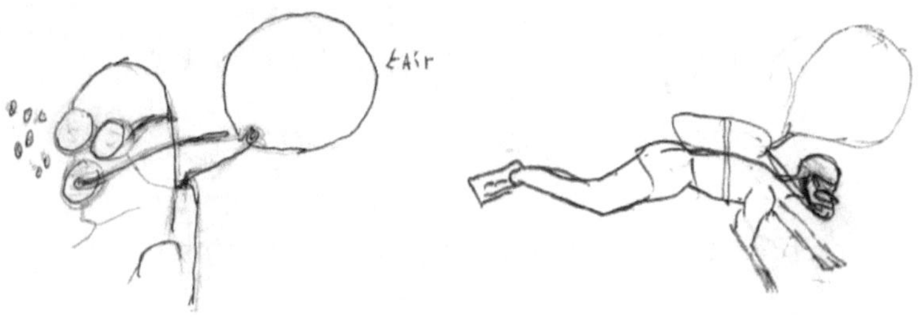

It has only been the last few months we have spent more time under the water. The next day we started searching the underwater city again, we found more statues and artwork, it was beautiful. We took some of the art to the surface we wanted to get a better look at it. The art was on metal plates, it had pictures of animals both from the land and sea. One of the plates had a picture of a large building; I think it may have been the courthouse or the main building of the city. There were a few plates with different being's on it: Human, Merbeing and some other type of being on it.

Tride and Tridax were a great help, I wish I had as much energy as they have! They carried some of the pots up to the surface for us to look at. Tride pointed out that there were Merbeings painted on the pots next to the humans. It looked like they were sharing a fish with the human, and the next pot also had three Merbeings on it, three in a row, on both sides of the pot, it was a much bigger pot, it looked like this:

The other one that they handed me looked like this:

Well I'm not the best artist, but we put the pots back after we looked at them. I wanted to make sure I didn't forget how they looked. I wanted to document that there was interaction between the Merbeings and Humans back then. I guess it is the history teacher in me!

The statues were mostly of animals and there were some drawings of trees on the walls. They were unusual looking trees, defiantly not from this area, so they must've seen them somewhere else. This city was built in a circular shape. The one on land was long; it goes from one side of the island to the other side. The city where the Roslanders live is also shaped in a circle, it has been rebuilt by the Merbeings and they had changed the shape somewhat, to make it easier for them to get around in it.

 **8** 

WE HAD ENJOYED exploring the underwater city that is on the other side of the island. It was the third part of the ancient city that we had found. You can tell that it was all connected at one time because of the artifacts that we have discovered through the years. After that last earthquake we had last month, we were pretty sure that's what happened to this city at one time. There must've been thousands of people living here, but now there are only us and the Roslanders.

We cannot go into the deeper water with our tanks because of the pressure, they won't work right. Tride has told us that there is a road of some type that goes out into the deeper water; but he is not sure where it is meant to go, because it just disappears. He also told us there are stones stacked on top of each other, which he assumes were buildings a very long time ago.

We would have loved to seen them in person, but the water is too deep. At least we can see them through Tride's eyes, when he connected to us. Tridax will even connect with us now and then. It is different seeing things through a child's eyes. He sees all the fish and holes in the walls, and he looks for things to do as he travels along. Trido and Tride are always looking out for danger and are not really looking to see all the wonders around them. Tridax bought us a beautiful stone and shells that he found in this one area he explored. We have never seen these types of stones or shells before. We told him we should investigate that area tomorrow, because we were done for the day, we are tired! He looked a little disappointed but understood, and swam off to join his dad.

Frank and Tride came up with the idea of using a raft to help with the diving. This way we can save our air and strength for diving instead of swimming out to the area and then diving. We can preserve our strength for swimming around in the ancient city. Tride and Tridax pulled the raft around the island for us, so we didn't have to carry it over the island on foot. I was very happy about that, we are in great shape but I think that would've been a little too much for me.

Tride pushed the raft to the shore for us so we could load up our tanks and nets. The raft wasn't very big. It was made for four people, but by the time we put our equipment on it, there wasn't that much room left for us, let alone any extra things. So we used the nets to carry any extra items on the side of the raft.

We headed out to meet the guys, and to our surprise Trigut, Tride wife, was there. I guess she wanted to hang out with her husband and son too! She had heard about the pots with the Merbeings on them, and she wanted to see them and maybe take them back to their city. She has always been very interested in our history and how we used to live with her people. She has been collecting old items from the different shipwrecks and taking them to their home (Castle) under the sea, for the people to see and learn more about both of our histories.

Trigut had shown me some of the things that they had been collecting, by connecting with us. There was a variety of art from all over the world. I don't have any idea where all of it had come from, but it is beautiful. She told me many pieces came from when the green ones were here. Some of the artwork was made out of gold and many pieces had been of Merbeings interacting with other beings. Not only humans, but the green ones too, were on some of the art. There were even some pictures with land creatures in them. There were statues of mermaids and mermen, standing together with little children next to them. I guess these are some of the beings I was told about from the ancient one.

 **9** 

ONCE WE GOT to the area where Tridax found the stones and shells we started looking around. Last night we had taken a closer look at the stones that he had given us the day before. There were red and green ones that you could see through. Frank and I had agreed they were sapphires and rubies. We were so surprised!

We didn't know what to expect when we looked in the area today. When we told Trido and Tride what the stones were, they were excited to see what else we would find. Maybe a treasure chest of jewels!

Tridax was leading the way, of course it didn't take him very long to get there, and Tridax was waving for us to hurry up. Once we arrived we saw a pile of jewels. Tridax had a necklace and Trigut also had a necklace she had put on, it even shined underneath the water. Tride had a crown in his hand, and Tridax was telling him to put it on. He looked at us and smiled and put it on his head. As we looked through the pile, it appeared like it had been in a treasure chest at one time. It also looked like there had been a shipwreck. So the jewels may not have been part of the ancient city. We loaded the jewels into the pots that we had also found and then put them into the nets. It was time for us to go to the surface we were getting low on air.

As we carried everything to the raft, we were excited about what we had discovered. We climbed into the raft and paddled it around the other side of the island, instead of trying to carry it across the land. Once we arrived at the bay and landed on shore, we started looking through all the things that we had discovered.

Trido and Esaw were waiting at the jetty for us. We all looked at the different things that we had brought back. Trigut wanted the pots that we had found earlier in the week, so Tride went back and got them. He also found a few other items that the Merbeings were on. Some of them had humans and Merbeings together, others had land animals with the Merbeing, which was even more unusual. There were some pots with sea animals on them too. Trigut wanted to keep the pots in their museum, in the castle in Utopia City.

Trido told us the pots with the fish on them were used by the humans to receive the fish from the Merbeings. They would trade for things that came from the land for the fish. The humans would leave the pots on the jetty and the mermen would put their catch in the pots and when they came the next time they would have a spear, knife or even fruit from the land. Whatever, they had agreed on before.

Trido pointed to one of the pots, "You see here, it is the name of the merman, he would put his fish in it, and they would know who it came from. Some of the pots were used for sea plants. There are many plants in the sea that helped heal the humans."

The Merbeing healer's would teach the human healers about these plants, what they did and how to use them. In return the humans would do the same for us." He said "This is how we knew what to get Aggie when she was ill. Our bodies are a lot alike, but there are some differences too. Some herbs that would help us can make you sicker or even kill you. The same with us, we have learned the hard way."

We had five of our people treated by a human healer, he continued, because at that time, the humans were having the same problem. So the humans treated them with the herbs that helped the humans, but instead the herb almost killed them. Luckily, one of our healers' arrived and saved them by giving them an herb that was good for Merbeings only. When we communicated with each other, we learned a lot, too bad things have changed, and it has to be the way it is now."

CHAPTER

10

T HE NEXT DAY we cleaned everything up, and it was agreed that the pots would go to their castle. We would keep the little the jewels; if we ever leave here we won't be hurting for money. Everything else we really didn't have any place to keep them, or have a need for them. After living here all these years we have discovered there is no point in keeping things that you can't use right away. We do have a few things decorating our house, but it is really not much.

After we finished cleaning everything out, we decided to go for a walk down the beach, it had been a while since we had done this. It was nice to be on land, instead of in the water. There were a lot of things on the beach more than normal. We walked over to the first pile of junk we saw and looked into the pile. At least we knew there wouldn't be a Merbeing in it, there hasn't been any storm for awhile.

It was full of normal things, seaweed, rope and netting. So we pulled out the netting and rope, which would be useful in the future. We would pick it up on our way back to the bay. Then we went to the next pile and it looked like the same old thing, but as we got closer we could see a box. It was metal, it was about 2' x 4' and it looked like it had been bounced around for a while, and it also had a lock on it. This meant we would have to take it back to the bay to open it. We pushed all of the junk off of it and it looked like it was in pretty good shape. There was no hole or breaks in it, which meant that whatever was inside was more than likely still good.

Frank hit the lock on the box with a piece of wood but it didn't come loose. Then Frank tried to pick it up but it was too heavy to carry all the way back to the bay. So we used the net and ropes that we had found to drag it home.

We put the box on the net and tied the rope to the net; we figure we would drag it back to the bay. We tested the rope, and it worked. It was getting dark; we figured we should head back. As we dragged the box, we noticed that the sand was building up in front of the box, making it harder to pull.

We stopped at the first pile and threw on the rest of the netting and rope that we had found earlier; we put it on top of the box. It wasn't easy pulling, because the sand would build up in front of the box, and we would have to stop and remove it again, and then we would drag it for another ten feet and then do it again.

By the time we got home it was dark and Trido's family had been watching us for a while. We had pulled the box up to the water's edge, and they all had big smiles on their faces. We weren't quite sure why, but we thought it was because we looked funny pulling a box down the beach.

Now all we had to do was figure out how to get the lock off. Frank headed up to the house to find whatever he could to help. After awhile he came back with some tools. It was dark by then; all we had was the moonlight to see what we were doing. Frank tried using our hammer, but it didn't work, then he tried a saw, still no luck! We were getting pretty tired we have had a long day. It was also getting pretty dark out; there was only a sliver of the moon out tonight. We decided to wait until the next day to try and get it open.

CHAPTER

11

OF COURSE, MOST of the night we were trying to come up with ideas on how to open the box. We figured out a couple different things that we would try. We didn't what to damage it; we also had plans for the box.

As we walked towards the bay the next morning, Trido and his family swam over to meet us. They were still smiling at us; we knew something was up so we finally asked them what they were smiling about?

Trido said "You know you could have pushed the box into the water and we could have helped pull it around to the bay for you, everything's lighter in the water. It would have been a lot easier then dragging it on the sand!"

Frank and I just looked at each other and smiled. Frank told Trido "You could've told us that earlier, but we will remember it for the next time!"

Another lesson learned!

The idea to open the box was to roll it on its side, to get a better angle at the lock. Then Frank would hit it with a hammer again, but this time we used a wedge in between the lock and the hammer. Frank struck it as hard as he could and the lock went flying off. We pushed it back onto its bottom and opened up the box. The anticipation of what could be in this box had been driving us nuts all night.

As Frank opened the metal box, we looked inside of it and there was a wooden chest. It was beautiful! Frank reached down to pull it out of the metal box, and you could tell it was handmade and had writing carved on top of it. I closed the metal box, so Frank could put the wooden chest on top of it. It was made out of a light wood with dark wood in between the light wood. There was a metal trim around the edges of the chest. On the front of it, the word Captain was carved on it.

I was a surprise to see the wooden chest inside the metal box. As Frank opened the wooden chest, we were all watching with anticipation to see what was inside. When we opened it, by the looks of it, it was all the things that the captain placed value on, and his own personal items. There was the Captain's journal, dueling pistols, a deck of cards, a few books, and pictures (I assume of his family), and a bottle of cognac with two glasses to go with it. The bottle and glass's were beautiful.

I felt that we were invading on his privacy, but curiosity got the better of us. We first looked at the Captains journal first. The captain's name was Gary Dean; he was the captain of his own ship. It looked like he chartered out to other people. The pictures were inside another smaller metal box in the chest, I guess to protect them. The pictures were of a woman and a little boy. There was a picture of an older couple, maybe his parents, and a picture of his dogs. There were two books besides the journal in the box, the first one was "How to fix things on a ship" book and the other one was Moby Dick. The deck of cards looked like they had been used quite a bit, but we could still use them. The dueling pistols looked very old and so did the cognac bottle and glasses that were in the chest.

We looked in his journal to see if there was any information about what had happened to the ship but there wasn't. The last log entry was a normal day at sea; he had chartered the boat out to three men to go fishing. According to the journal they hadn't gotten anything in three days, and that was the last entry in the journal. The rest of the information in the journal we felt was just his personal business, so we aren't going to write anything else about it in my journal.

Maybe someday if we get off this island we can look him up and give him back his journal. Although trying to find a Gary Dean in the United States may be a challenge, if he's even still alive.

We offered Trido and his family a drink of the cognac but they said no thank you. Which brought up a subject that we had never really asked them about, do they drink alcohol?

Trido replied "Not your kind of alcohol, we do have drinks that affect us like alcohol affects humans. The human alcohol makes us very sick and dries our bodies out."

Frank replied back "That makes sense, so I guess we get to keep the cognac for ourselves!"

Frank started putting the items back into the chest, so we could take it up to the house; we knew the wooden chest was fairly light, but the metal box was much heavier. We wanted to keep the metal box as a storage unit; it took us two trips to get them both up to the house.

We decided to take another walk down the beach, just to enjoy the night air. Hopefully we wouldn't find anything else at this point, it seemed like every time we went out we discovered something new. For being a deserted island there sure was a lot to be discovered.

It was a warm night, with a light breeze, all you could hear was the ocean and the animals in the forest. As we were walking along we saw movement in the water, then we saw them, it was dolphins playing, jumping into the air and riding on their tails. It was fun to watch, our own private show. They swam off toward the bay, and we continued to walk along the beach. It's funny how young I felt, walking hand and hand with the man I love. I guess Frank could hear what I was thinking; he looked at me and smiled and squeezed my hand. As night started to fall, we headed back to the bay. As we got closer, we could see the dolphins still playing in the bay, they had come to visit the Roslanders.

The younger children were watching the older children doing acrobats with the dolphins. The teenagers were having fun, trying their luck at tail riding and doing flips, they were pretty good. We watched for a little while, and then Frank said "Can I buy you a drink?" I hadn't heard that in a long time. I replied "Well yes sir you can!"

We went to the house, and opened up the bottle of Cognac from Captain Gary Dean's chest. We raised our glasses that were from the chest, and thanked the Captain for the drinks. All I can say is it was really good! Frank said "This is a really high class Cognac!" I wouldn't know I have never had cognac before. This was another first on the island for me.

12

THE NEXT MORNING we got up and did things around the house for awhile, we even did some cleaning, well as much as you can with a dirt floor and plants growing inside and outside your home. We even have wild chickens around, if you feed them, they will hang out by your home. It makes it much easier to catch them. We also have a couple of pigs as pets. If you notice, I called them pets. Originally we were going to keep them penned up, so that way we wouldn't have to chase them when we wanted to have pork. But we never got around to eating them, so after a few months they became our pets. Their names are Fido and Rex! We miss our dogs so we figured why not a couple pigs as pets instead. The only thing is they even come to their names. Maybe, not the right name but they do come to us when we call.

We also filled up our water tank with the freshwater that we get from the creek, which is next to our house. Normally, the creek is high enough to fill the tank but sometimes it gets low so we have to manually fill the tank. The tank came from our sailboat; the Roslanders were nice enough to get it out for us. They also got our toilet from the wreckage. We may use an outhouse but at least we have a toilet to sit on. There is a lot of wood and other miscellaneous stuff always washing up on the beach, so we always have material to build things and create new items.

We even have running water kind of! Frank has come up with a bucket and he hangs it over the sink (well it's kind of a sink, it's just another bucket) so after I wash the dishes in the first bucker, I can wash the dishes off with the bucket that hangs above the sink, it works pretty good. Granted we don't have a lot of dishes and we use our fingers quite a bit these days.

After we got our chores done we decided to go down to the bay and see what was going on there. This is our normal routine here on the island, we get our chores done then we go down to the bay and visit with the Roslanders. We do some fishing, and sometimes we will go out into the bay and get clams and different sea urchins and sea plants to eat. I call everything sea urchins these days because we had no clue what kind of shellfish we are eating!

Just because you're on a deserted island doesn't mean you don't have work to do. If you want to survive in this environment you have to get a routine in place, and make sure that you have enough water and food to live on. We are lucky enough to have the Roslanders to help us when we need it, but we do try not to intrude on their lives. We treat them as family, and try not to get in the way too much.

Today they are getting ready to do their migration, so they are very busy getting things put away and hidden, so there is no proof that they were ever here. As Trido has told us many times you never know when the island may be discovered by other humans. So we sat on the jetty and watched as they moved about and got things ready to go.

Tridax came over to visit with us, and gave us both a necklace that he had made. He said "This is for you to remember me by while I am gone." They were beautiful and we thanked him and told him that we wouldn't forget him no matter what! He swam off to be with his parents and waved at us as he dived into the water.

Frank turned to me and said "He is becoming quite the little diver isn't he?" I just smiled and said yes!

I asked Frank, so what adventure we are going on this time while they are gone.

Frank replied back "How do you feel about hiking to the other end of the island and seeing what's over there?"

That sounded good to me, it gave us something new to do! So we started making a list of all the things that we would need to take with us, because it will take at least a couple of weeks to go on this adventure. The good news is we really didn't have to carry that much food but we did need to carry water because we were not sure about the freshwater on that end of the island.

I told Frank we need to tell the Roslanders where we will be going just in case something happens. He agreed, so he waved at Tride to come over. Tride swam over to us, and we agreed on a signal that we would put in the bay house if we were rescued while they were gone.

We told Tride about our plan to go to the other end of the island and that we would take all of the items out of the bay house if for some reason we got rescued from here. Tride agreed that was a good idea; because if they came back and we weren't here they wouldn't know if we were hurt or if we had been rescued.

We told him to tell his family to have a good journey and that we would see them when they got back. As he swam off he smiled and waved, and then turned and did a tail ride backward. What a show off!

As the Roslanders headed out to sea, we headed back to the house to pack for the trip tomorrow. When we got to the house we turned to wave good-bye again, but they were gone.

13

WE HAD EVERYTHING packed for the trip. We wanted to leave early while the tide was out, that way we wouldn't have to travel around the mountain, and through the forest. It would save us a day, granted it really didn't matter, what else did we have to do?

The next morning, as we were headed out, the sun was just coming up. The sky was beautiful, not a cloud to be seen. But that didn't mean there couldn't be a storm by that night. We went around the cliff, and we could see the tide was still out. We could see where the cavern was, where we first saw the Roslanders. That is where they go when there is a big storm coming in. We normally just stay in our house by the tree line. It is made out of stacked rocks, so a tree could fall on it and we would be safe. We have been in the cavern a few times, but it feels like it belongs to them and we shouldn't be in there. I don't know why we just do!

As we rounded the corner, all we could see was the beach. The island has a nice beach that is a couple miles long, on the one side. When we were over at the underwater city (city number three) which is on the other side we couldn't see the end of the island. We had investigated the other side of the island earlier in our arrival here, but we had never gone all the way to the other end of the island. But we will this time.

We had packed our sleeping bags, and a couple of tarps, and some spears and fishing poles. Of course my turtle bowl, as much as I hated killing the turtle, it is the best bowl I have ever had. The sleeping bags are starting to look their age, so is everything else, but it all still works!

We had made it about half way when we stopped for the night; we were at the first place we had stayed, when we landed here. The sign from the boat that we had left here on a tree was still there. The storage area that Frank had made was all filled in by sand and trees. If it wasn't for the sign I wouldn't have ever known we were there.

As we set up camp, Frank went and caught a couple of fish, and I found some nice plants to eat, ones that we knew were safe to eat. We had just finished our meal, when we saw a pod of whales going by. They had a couple of babies with them, and were making calls to each other. The babies were playing, and jumping in and out of the water. Then all of a sudden one of the bigger whales came up out of the water, clearing his whole body and did a turn and dived back into the water. It was beautiful! The babies stopped long enough to watch and then they tried to do it. They did get about half their bodies out of the water. This time of year we saw a lot of different sea life. They were all migrating, to their breeding grounds. We watched for awhile and then pretty soon they were out of sight. Frank asked if I wanted to play some cards, and of course I said yes. Our own cards had worn out a couple of months ago, so it was another thank you to Captain Gary Dean.

While we played another round of the card game Spite and Malice, we started planning our next day. We didn't know if we could go around the point or if we would be going through the forest. Frank said, "Well, when we are ready to go and the tide is out, we'll try the point and then we'll come back through the forest."

It sounded like a good plan to me. We settled in under our tarp, and watched the sky; there were so many stars out there. We always put up a tarp to sleep under: you never knew what kind of weather you would wake up to this time of year.

As we watched there was so much action, stars shooting from one side of the sky to the other. The sky was as clear as it had been all day. We found all the constellations that we knew of and a few that we discovered. The moon was almost full, so you could see as if it was daylight. I wondered if our kids were looking up at the sky right now wondering if they were doing the same thing. Good night Kids!

14

UP AND AT it, as Frank would say! He had caught breakfast last night, so we had leftover fish and eggs with a side of sea plant for breakfast. The eggs we had gotten from our chickens that live with us. Frank had made a carrying pouch for them; it was padded so they wouldn't crack as we traveled.

The tide was out so it meant that we would be going around the mountain, instead of going into the forest today. As we got to the other side of the mountain there was another long beach ahead of us. This was the first time that we had seen this side of the island, since our arrival here. We had seen it when we were on the raft but we ended up on the other side of the mountain, thanks to the Roslanders.

There were a few clouds in the sky, but we didn't think it was anything to worry about; we would just keep an eye on them. There was a lot of debris on the beach, as we walked along we would check each of the piles to see if there was anything of value for us to come back for later. We felt like we were the keepers of the beach, we would try to keep it as clean as we could whenever we could.

As usual there were a lot of nets, ropes and a few sea creatures that had gotten caught up in the nets and died. Of course there were tons and tons of seaweeds, but nothing you would want to eat.

We decided it was time to take a break and have lunch. And you'll never guess what we had for lunch? You're right, fish! The good news is the different types of fish that we had caught, did have a different flavor from each other.

After lunch we packed up and headed down the beach, when we saw something moving. We approached it very cautiously, because you never know what you'll find. As we got closer, we could tell there was more than one of them. There was about a dozen seals, laying out and enjoying the sun. They could care less about us they raised their heads and shook them, then went back to sunbathing. We decided to keep our distance anyway, there's nothing worse than a pissed off seal.

As we walked along we would look out into the ocean hoping to see some unusual rock formations, but at that point we hadn't seen anything. We decided to go into the forest and see if there was any kind of formations or any ancient ruins to be found. We set up camp before we headed into the forest that way we would have everything set up when we returned for the night. Normally, by the end of the day we were exhausted, after we do these exploring things. It didn't take long to set up the camp, mostly because there wasn't much to do. We always left the sleeping bags rolled up until it was time for bed. You never know what might crawl into them!

Frank took the lead as we went into the woods; he had the machete so he was clearing a path as we went. This was another way for us not to get lost; we would always make sure there was a path coming from the direction that we entered. Granted if you're on an island sooner or later you're going to run into the ocean. If you get injured though, you want to know the quickest route to get back to camp. This is how you think when you have been married to a retired soldier for 40 years. It definitely not a bad thing!

15

FRANK WAS ABOUT fifteen feet ahead of me when all of a sudden he disappeared. He didn't yell or anything, he just disappeared, so I started yelling his name and I heard nothing. What the heck happened to him! I wasn't sure what to do, so I walked slowly towards where I last saw him. As I got closer to where he was last seen, I could hear his voice. He was yelling to stay back; there was a big hole he had fallen into.

I walked very cautiously up to the hole, which now was big enough to see and turned my flashlight on, and sure enough there was Frank. I thought for sure my heart was going to jump out of my chest, but once I saw him everything was okay. The good news is we did have a rope, so all those years of collecting rope came in handy again.

I tried one end of the rope to a tree and threw down the other end to Frank. As he climbed up the rope, he kept talking but I couldn't understand what he was saying. So once he came out of the hole I asked him what he was talking about.

Frank said "There's a tunnel down there, it looks like a long tube. It's carved out of the rock, it looks man-made, and it is smooth and straight. What to guess what we will be doing for the next couple of days?"

I just smiled at him and nodded my head, and replied "We're going to need more rope!

Frank said "There is some water not deep at all it, must have come from the rain the other night. He couldn't see the end of the tube, but it was big enough for us to walk in, and it was clean. It had no roots or cracks from what he could see."

New plan, we need to go back to camp to get our extra battery for the flashlight, matches, water, all the rope we can carry, and a couple of spears. It's always good to be prepared!

The plan was to use the rope that was tied to the tree, and follow the tunnel, as far as we could. Then, we could pull the rope out and see how long the tunnel was. We had no idea what the tunnel was. The Ancient one did say the Green ones used tunnels to get around.

We went back to the beach and got all of our supplies together and headed back to the hole and the tunnel we had found. It was really dark inside the tunnel: having second thoughts I turned to Frank and asked him "Are you sure?"

He replied "Yes, ladies first!"

I headed for the opening and Frank grabbed me and said "Smart Butt" then he went down the rope first. After he got to the bottom I threw him our supplies, and then I went down the hole. It was about ten feet deep, and the air wasn't bad. It felt like there was air flowing from where we entered the tunnel. There was only water where the hole was, after about five feet it was dry. As we walked I put my hands on the walls. They were smooth and there were no cuts or lines, it is as if it was one whole unit, just one long tube. We did find some lamp looking things, but we couldn't tell how they worked. We decided to take one back to camp with us, so we could check it out and see how it worked. The tunnel had a round ceiling, and the floor was nice and flat. We couldn't tell when the last time someone had used the tunnel. I could have swept the floor and it would have looked like it was new.

We walked for awhile, until we could see another tunnel going off to the right, it had stairs going up. The stairs looked like any other stone stairs going up to someone's house. There looked to be about twenty of them. It was hard not to go see what was at the end of them, but there was another tunnel going straight, and we could see some light. We wanted to see where the light was coming from, so we went straight.

As we got closer to the light we could hear the ocean and the air was fresher. Then the tunnel just opened up and we were on the beach again. It was weird we just walked right out of it, and we were on the other side of the island. It was the area where we had found the small huts a few years ago. We could see them from the tunnel, but the tunnel opening was covered with vegetation, so you really couldn't see it from the beach.

It only took us three hours to get to the other side of the island, using the tunnel. It wasn't hard work at all; it was pretty straight the whole time.

It was getting dark so we set up camp for the night. We decided we wanted to check the area out a little more. I could tell this was going to take a lot longer than two weeks. I made a fire while Frank went and caught a couple of fish. He did find some nice clams, so I heated up some water. We had fish and clam soup for dinner. Add a few herbs and you'd have a $30 meal at a restaurant. Well maybe $20, anyway Frank said it was a nice change!

We looked at the lamp we found, and it had oil in it still. So we poured a little of it out on a piece of wood, and lit it. The oil started right up. Then we got brave and lit the lamp. It gave off a wonderful glow, so we knew it would be safe to use inside the tunnel. We let it burn from a while just to make sure that it was safe. There were at least ten more of the lamps inside the tunnel and we had plenty of matches too. We blew out the lamp and settled into the bed of leaves that we had made, the sleeping bags were still at the first camp. We watched the stars until we fell asleep, no cards tonight.

16

WHEN I WOKE up, Frank was gone. I got up and looked around, I thought maybe he was on the beach, so I called for him, and there was no answer. I had a funny feeling I knew where he had gone, the tunnel! So I walked over to the entry way and yelled "FRANK" "FRANK are you in there?"

As he came out of the darkness, he had one of the lamps with him. All he said was "What?"

I replied "You couldn't wait for me?"

Frank said "You were sleeping so good, I figured I would light some of the lamps and see how much light they would give off. They give off a lot of light, it was almost day light in there. You ready to go?'

I asked him "Wouldn't you like to eat before we pack up and head into the tunnel again?"

He acted surprised and said, "Oh yea, sure!"

We had the rest of the fish and clam soup. No point in dumping it. We cleaned and packed up our equipment, we had no idea where we would end up tonight!

We headed back into the tunnel, Frank had left every other lamp burning all the way to the staircase, that we had seen yesterday. It was a lot faster to travel than before, because for once we knew where we were going. The lamps were nice and bright. It was also nice, we knew we didn't have to watch out for anything and we could move at a faster pace. As we walked along we could see writing on the walls and pictures. We couldn't see them yesterday because all we had were our flashlights. With the lamps all glowing it was really easy to see the writing and pictures. The pictures were of different animals on the island and also others that we hadn't seen here, but are known on the outside world. There were also pictures of sea creatures. They were unusual looking creatures; they resembled some of the dinosaur pictures I had seen in books. As we looked closer, we could see that there was writing on the walls next to the animals (maybe the names of them)! We had no clue what the writing said, but it was unusual looking. I have never seen any type of writing like this before.

These are just a few of the sea creatures that we saw on the walls

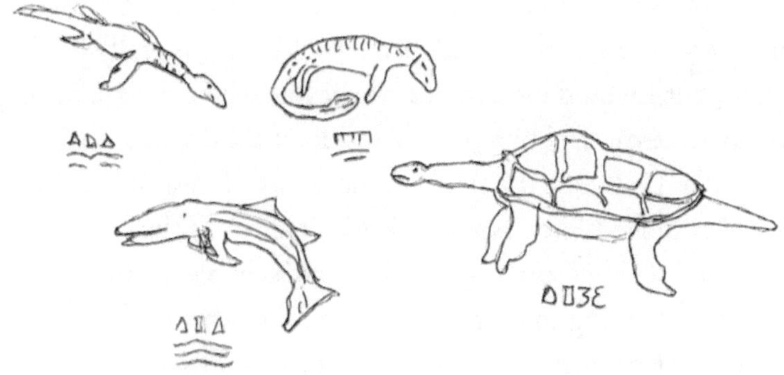

We started going up the steps, and as we got closer to the top you could see the light reflecting off of something. Both sides of the staircase were also glowing. It looked like there was light coming from the room above. This really didn't make any sense to us, so we decide to be very cautious as we moved up the staircase.

We came out of the staircase and there was a huge room, the ceiling was about eight feet high and there were holes, about ten inches wide, they were letting the light in from the ceiling. There were other holes on the sidewall about six feet from the floor. As we walked closer to the holes on the sidewall you could feel the air coming through them. Then as I walked around we saw other rooms, around the edge of the main floor. The floor was a light green and dark green resembling grass and the ceiling was a baby blue, like the sky. If we didn't know better I would think we were outside. There was art on the walls; it looked a lot like the forest outside, but it also had drawings of different things, we really couldn't tell at this point what it was.

Frank lit a few more of the lamps that were on the walls. As we looked in the different rooms there was art work of different sceneries from around the world. It was beyond being beautiful! Much of the scenery I had seen in books or in our travels across the United States.

As you walked into the side rooms, you had the feeling that you were walking into another place and time. It is really hard to explain, but I would have to describe it like when you are having a dream, but you feel like you are inside of the dream.

I walked into one room where there was a forest, it had white trees, that looked like, Aspen, I think that's what they are called and I could see deer standing around, and a couple of rabbits. The leaves were turning into autumn colors, the most beautiful reds and orange with just a little bit of green. I could swear that they were moving as I stood there. I felt like the deer were watching me as I walked around the room. Also their heads and tails had moved. The rabbits wiggled their noses, and had moved away from me, but continued to watch me. I would have sworn I was there in that forest with them!

Frank had gone into another room and his room was a desert, with an ancient city just in the horizon. It had a couple of camels and other desert animals. He said "That it was the same with him; it was as if he was in the desert. It was hot and he could smell the camels. As he moved towards the picture he could feel he was getting closer to the city." Then he heard me call for him, so he came out of the room and joined me out in the middle of the theater room. He asked why I called him and I told him I was just wondering where you were at.

We continued to go into the different rooms and each of them did the same thing, each room had a different painting, with different scenery in it. It was like stepping into another place and time, where you could enjoy the environment and feel like you were really there. It was really weird, but I could see how the people that made this would enjoy it. All of the sceneries were made to make you feel good, and even the animals big and small were friendly.

We came back out into the center of the big room, and we noticed there was a hallway leading off into another direction. We decided to camp in this room for the night and explore the next area tomorrow.

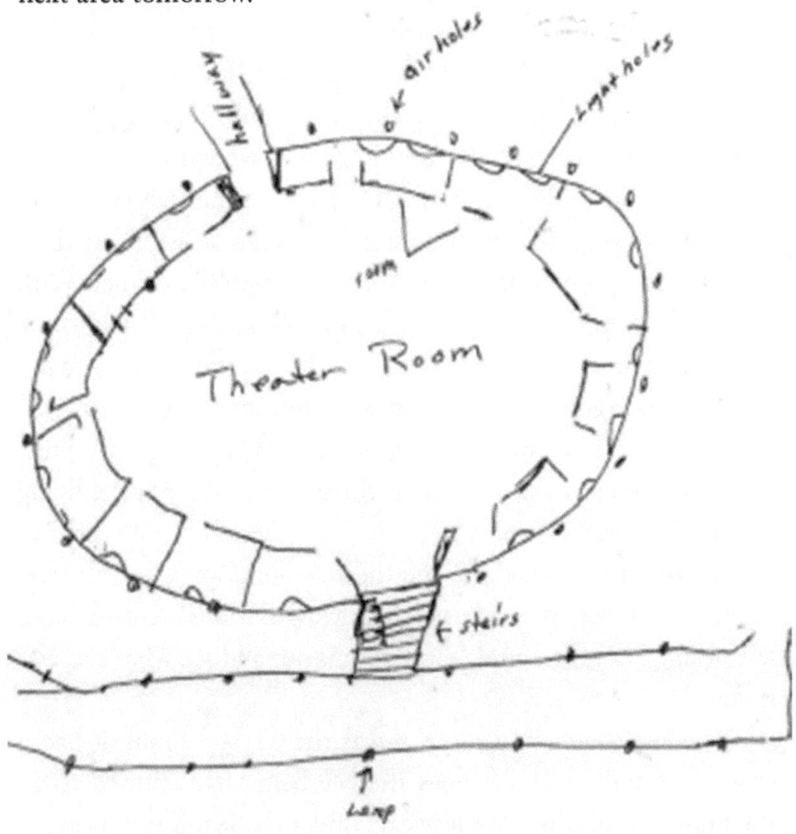

As we settled in for the night, we continued to explore the theater room (this is what we ended up calling it). There was writing on the walls, and pictures of Humans and the Green Ones. By the looks of it the Merbeings didn't come into this area. I would assume it's because there is no water way into the mountain, and it would really be hard for them to get into this area, from the sea.

I wished that I had a camera so I could have taken lots of pictures, but even if I had a camera at that point I'd be out of film! Neither Frank nor I are very good at drawing pictures but we do try to capture as much as we can, you never know someday, someone may find these journals.

We decided that it would be a good idea for us to go to our first campsite and get our sleeping bags and other equipment, it wasn't that far away. By the looks of it we will be spending a couple days inside the mountain. By the time that we got to the first campsite the sun was starting to set, so we hurried up and packed up our stuff and headed back into the tunnel. With the lamps lit in the tunnel it didn't take long to get back to the staircase. You could hear the sounds of the ocean and the wind blowing through the tunnel, and we could smell the ocean air.

Frank and I had been talking about what type of people must have lived here, by the looks of it, there hasn't been anyone living here for hundreds of years.

As we arrived back into the theater room, we set up the rest of our camp, which was basically putting out our sleeping bags. We decided to try a couple more rooms out and see what else was there.

The last room we went into was the Crystal room, it had a cave of crystals, like the ones the Merbeing had showed us in their communication, but it wasn't under the sea, it was a cavern on land somewhere. You could feel the crystals glowing and the energy coming from them. The longer we stood there the more we felt a part of them. Then Frank said "We need to leave!" For a moment I didn't understand why, and then I could feel my legs starting to hurt. It was weird, I felt like I was becoming part of the room.

Once we got out of the room, everything was fine; I turned to Frank and asked what was happing in there?

Frank replied "I don't know, but when I looked at you, you looked like you were not here anymore, it scared me, and that's why I told you, we needed to leave."

I understood what he said; I did feel like I was walking inside the cavern, touching the stones, feeling their power. It was wonderful, I didn't want to leave, but I'm glad he pulled me out of the dream.

We didn't know it but a lot of time had gone by. We needed to get more food, for some reason the food we had, had all dried out. We went out to the first camping area we had stayed at earlier. The plan was to come back and check out the hallway we had found. But we needed to get more food, we needed to go fishing and gather more plants to eat. After we got our food supplies filled, we would come back in and check out the hallway and anything else that may be there.

It was a beautiful night out so we decide to stay out on the beach tonight. As we watched the moon come up, it was almost full. I turned to Frank, and said, wasn't it a half moon when we went into the tunnel?

He nodded his head in agreement. Then he replied "What happened? We were only in there for a day, so why is the moon full now?"

It must be the rooms! It must be some kind of time displacement. We went into the: Mountain range, Redwood forest, Wheat fields, Valleys, Ocean Cliffs and the underwater rooms. I didn't think we stayed more than ten minutes in each of the rooms. But if the moon is right, then we spent almost a day in each of the rooms. No wonder we're so hungry and the food was all dried up! Funny how things really don't surprise us anymore!

As we settled in for the night, we started talking about the different rooms; I decided to call them dream rooms. As we talked about each of the rooms, we found we were seeing different things too. For example in the Redwood forest, I saw the large trees; and there were deer and bears just wandering around. I could hear birds singing and other animals calling to each other. While Frank saw the large trees, and different animals. He also saw a tree house with a rope going up to it. He climbed it and could see the fields in the distance. He has always wanted a tree house, and what better place than in a tall Redwood forest!

It was the same for each of the rooms, it would start out as just a picture of some place and then your dreams would come to life. Whatever, you would be thinking of; the room would make it feel like it was really happening. There was no violence or death, it was a lot like heaven would be, I think.

I think we could have talked for hours, but it was time to get some sleep, we hadn't slept in a week.

WHEN WE WOKE up it was mid-day, this was a first for us. We could have slept even longer but the sun was beating down on us. We ate and talked about what to do next, and we agreed to just hang out on the beach for the day, and catch up on our rest. We still felt exhausted and needed to get some fresh water. There was a creek not too far from where we were camping. I went off to get some water and plants to eat, Frank went to the water's edge with his pole to try and catch some fish. After we ate, and drank lots of water, we were just laying there on our sleeping bags, when the next thing we knew it was morning.

We couldn't believe it! We slept most of a whole day away again. But we did feel better; so we drank the rest of the water. I got up to get more, and I turned to Frank and told him "Don't fall asleep while I'm gone!" When I returned he just said "I'm still awake!" I replied, good for you! So what are we going to do now?

Frank said, "Well one thing is we're not going in the dream rooms together again, if we go in them at all."

I agreed it was too dangerous for us to be in the rooms together, we had no control over time. It was weird, I felt like the rooms were calling for us to come back, when I told Frank, and he said he had the same feeling.

It was around noon when we went back into the tunnel; we wanted to see where the hallway went. As we were going up the stairs we could feel the rooms calling to us. We knew their secrets now though, and we were not going into them again. Well at least not together! We walked through the theater room and headed down the hallway. We lit every other lamp on the wall, as we walked down the hall. It seemed strange, the hallway shouldn't have been that long, and we could also see other doorways, in the distance. The hallway was the same as the theater room it had green and brown coloring on the floor and the ceiling was a baby blue, with clouds painted in. It was mirroring the outside world.

On the walls there were trees and rocks painted a lot like a forest going down to the ocean. When we came to the first room, there were no doors on the rooms; everything was built out of the stones inside of the mountain. What I would assume were beds, were built into the wall. They were pretty comfortable too, which was unusual because it was stone. It felt cold but yet warm on my back at the same time. I told Frank to lie down and see if he got the same results, he did. I didn't tell him what I felt because I wanted to see if it would be the same thing for him.

As he lay inside the hole, he wasn't sure what to expect, because of the way I acted in it. But as he laid there he seemed to be enjoying it, so I asked him well what do you think?

He replied "Nice, maybe we should stay here tonight!"

I told him I don't think so after the dream rooms I'm not sure what would happen if we laid in these beds for the night.

He jumped out of the bed, and said "Oh yeah maybe it wouldn't be a good idea."

Each of the rooms that we went into was the same they only had one color from top to bottom. One room was completely baby blue, another was a light green and another was a red. In each of the rooms you could feel the different energy from the colors. The last room on the this level, was yellow, like the sun, when we walked into it we could feel the heat/energy coming from it, when we left that room we were ready to do a marathon, because we had so much energy.

We continued to walk down the hallway; it seemed to be sloping down as we walked. Then it turned and there was another whole area. I would assume underneath the other rooms. These rooms were not as elaborate as the one above us; they look more like living quarters than anything else. There was a living room, what I would call a dining room and then bedrooms on the side. They were all nice size; you could live very comfortable in this space. The temperature was just right, from what I could see who ever lived here didn't eat or drink anything, or they did it outside of the mountain, because I didn't see any kind of kitchen. Which would be weird? "Right?"

We went down another flight of stairs, and this time it was a large room with pillars throughout it.

Frank said "That is probably what holds up everything else above us." We saw a little chamber in the wall, with pots of some kind in the hole. I think this is their mausoleum, and the pots held their remains. Frank looked inside one of the pots, there was only ash inside. Each of them had writing on it; I assume it was their name on the pot. There were rows, after rows of the holes in the wall, it went around the room and was five high. Every one of them had a pot. There was something different about this room; it felt like we shouldn't be there. It was very uncomfortable, so I headed toward the door and Frank was right behind me.

As we walked to the end of the room we could see a staircase going up. Frank said "What the heck?" As we headed up the staircase it brought us back to the tunnel that we originally came through, in the beginning.

We have no clue what this building was or who lived here. I really don't know what else to call it, so I'm going to call it a building in my journal. It was amazing how all of the walls and floors had no tool marks on them; it was as smooth on the floor as it was on the walls and ceiling too.

Since we were in the tunnel we decided it was time to head out to the beach and get some food and water. The bizarre thing is, (well one of the bizarre things), is that we didn't see the staircase that we just came out of earlier. We had gone the length of the tunnel earlier and we only saw the one staircase as we walked through the first time. But there are two staircases both coming from different floors, but ending in the tunnel.

As we were walking back to the campsite, we were passing the first staircase we found, and the dream rooms were calling to us. We looked at each other, and said what the heck! We'll take turns and we can only stay in the room for thirty minutes, we turned and went up the stairs. I told Frank you go first, I'll come get you in thirty minutes. I asked him which room you are going into; he didn't have to think twice, the forest with the Redwood trees!

He asked me "Which one are you going to pick?" I told him. I think the cliff that is looking over the valley.

Frank left and went into the room; as I was waiting, I started looking at the art work on the walls. From what I know about history, the art work came from different time periods, almost a hundred years apart, if not more. I looked at a section, and it looked like it came from Greece in the early 1500 and in another section the art and writing was from the 1800, not sure where, I haven't seen this type of writing before. If I could read the writing, I think it would be telling me, the history of the people that lived here at one time. As the pictures changed from one section to the other so did the writing, as if the writing was advancing.

I was so involved with the wall I almost forgot about getting Frank out of the room. I walked into the room, and the look in his eyes, you could tell he was far away and enjoying whatever he was doing. I really hated pulling him away from wherever he was. But when I touched him, he returned to me immediately. First thing he said "Has it been thirty minutes already?"

I told him it is more like forty minutes, I was side tracked looking at the walls. How was your dream?

Frank said "Let's go out to the main room and talk, this room is trying to pull me back into my dream." We left the room and I waited for him to tell me about his dream.

"It's hard to believe I was only in there for forty minutes. I did so much. I walked around the forest, and I could smell the redwoods. I could see the sun trying to break through the trees. The wild life was everywhere; they even came up to me, and let me touch them. I haven't seen trees that big since I was a little boy, living in California. My brother and I would go with our parents to the Redwood Forest and hook our hands together around a tree and we would barely reach each other. Every year we would try to reach each other, it was how we could tell we were growing. It was a wonderful time in my childhood. The forest was full of sounds, from the wind blowing in the trees, to the animals calling to each other. I even heard the woodpecker drilling into the trees, it was amazing."

I don't think I've ever seen Frank with that look on his face before; he looked like a little boy that had just had a wonderful adventure. Then he caught himself and came back to being good old Frank!

It's pretty amazing how these dream rooms work. I'm sure you could get lost in there forever if you wanted. Frank asked "Are you ready to go into your dream?"

I was kind of nervous after seeing how Frank came out of the dream, but I was really looking forward to being back in Utah, where I had grown up. The painting in the dream room I'm sure wasn't Utah but it was close enough to home, I figured I'd give it a shot. As I was headed to the room I turned and saw Frank looking really tired and so I asked him "Are you going to be able to stay awake and come get me in thirty minutes?"

He responded by saying "Yes, but I think I'm going to go out to the beach and get some fresh air, I need to get some water too. I will be back in thirty minutes to get you out of there."

That made me feel a little bit safer, because once you leave this area it doesn't have the hold it has on you while you are inside. As I walked into the dream room I could feel it pulling me into the dream, within seconds I was on the cliff in Utah.

The cliff was overlooking a large valley, and it was all red stones and as the sun hit the walls of the Valley, it looked like it was on fire. It was as gorgeous as I remembered it from when I was a child. I could see the eagles flying overhead and herds of elk down in the Valley. As I stood on top of the cliff I could hear the calls of the difference animals. The elk were singing and yelling at another herd farther down in the Valley and they were responding back. The eagles were also screaming, and enjoying the airflow in the Valley. It was a gorgeous day there was a light breeze. As I wandered along the edge of the cliff I saw a herd of deer, and some cattle in a field. I could even see an old homestead in the distance, with smoke coming out of the chimney. This is so real it's kind of scary, but as I stood there I could feel myself being a part of the scene instead of just watching. I found a path going down the cliff side and decided to take it. As I walked down the path I continued to watch the action in the valley below. The path looked like it was made by the animals that lived here, and it was used a lot. It was easy to travel down, as I got closer to the different herds, there were horse, elk, deer and cattle, but they all seem to move away, as I got closer. They continued to move around and to speak to each other, and then all of a sudden I was back in the room with Frank. I couldn't believe it had only been thirty minutes.

"Welcome back, how was your dream?" Frank asked.

I replied, "It was wonderful; it was just like I remembered when I was a child in Utah. The colors, the sounds and the feeling of peace you feel when you're sitting on top of a mountain.

What an amazing place these dream rooms are. It wouldn't have been hard to stay in this dream forever. I'm really glad we hadn't found this place before now; if we would have found this place first we would've never left it, and then we would've never met the Roslanders! We could have been lost in here forever. Frank agreed and we decided that we wouldn't be coming back here again; it was just too dangerous for us.

CHAPTER

W E WALKED OUT of the tunnel and Frank had asked me for more details about my dream and I told him everything. I told him about the wonderful Valley, and all the wonderful wildlife. The eagles were the biggest I've ever seen and the herds were very large.

If we ever get rescued I think I want to go back and visit Utah again. Maybe we will take a trip to Utah and then to California, and you can see your redwoods once again. I told him.

Frank said "That would be a great idea let's make a plan and do it. Maybe we can take the kids and their families too!"

As we walked out onto the beach the first thing we had to do is get water, we had been inside for quite a while. Frank and I both walked over to the spring and got the water. We decided to take a walk on the beach, and take a swim in the bay, maybe we could find some sea urchins to eat for dinner.

Frank said "He was out wandering around waiting for me to finish my dream. He did see a couple chickens that looked pretty good!" Well if you want chicken, you're goanna have to go catch them! I said. He just laughed and said "Maybe I'll do that."

We floated for awhile in the bay and enjoyed the day, then went up to the sleeping bags and took a nap. When I woke up, Frank had a chicken cooking over the fire. It smelled good. I guess he wanted chicken after all!

After we ate and cleaned up, we played some cards and I wanted to update my journal. While I was writing in my journal, Frank went for a walk in the forest, I told him to watch out for any more holes. He lifted up a long stick and said "I got it covered!"

He was gone longer than normal, so I called out his name, just to check on him, and he replied "What?" He scared the heck out of me; he was standing right behind me. As I turned he was standing there, smiling and laughing at me. Not funny! What have you been doing?

I found some more ancient buildings; it looks like it might be a part of the mountain building. This place must have been huge, even bigger than the ancient city on our side of the island.

I didn't know what to say, except I guess we'll be investigating here for awhile, the Roslanders won't be back for another month or so anyway. I guess if you have to be stranded on an island, this is a great one to land on.

I have been watching a storm front coming in for awhile, and I have been moving everything back into the woods for protection. I pointed out to sea, and Frank looked out and said "Yea, I saw it earlier; it looks like it is going to be a big one. Hopefully, it will change course and not hit us straight on."

After about an hour, you could tell the storm was going to hit us straight on, we decide to head for the tunnel, for protection. We gathered up as much as we could, and headed toward the tunnel. By now the wind was really starting to pick up, and you could see the heavy rain not too far from the shore line.

Frank yelled "Run!" Which I did! We threw everything into the hole, and I grabbed the rope and jumped down, and Frank was almost on top of me. The rain hit, it was like hail stones, but they were just really big rain drops. We could hear trees falling and the wind howling from the ocean. We walked to the other end of the tunnel to watch the storm, because we couldn't see anything from this side of the tunnel. Because we were in a hole we couldn't look out. The storm was just starting to hit this side of the island.

The clouds were grey and black, and we could see the lightening inside the clouds, there was a yellow and orange glow inside the clouds. Then lines of lightening would go across the sky, it was reminiscent of a spider web and then the lightening would come from another direction. It was as if the gods were fighting over the ocean, as the lightening went back and forth against each other. The clouds looked almost like they were rolling over each other, then the rain started. It was a driving rain; we have seen this type of rain in Texas, many times.

As we stood in the mouth of the tunnel, we could see the waves they were so high it looked like the ocean was trying to touch the sky. The sky was shooting lightning bolts back at the ocean trying to reach it. It was a battle of power, and beautiful to watch. It was much better to enjoy the storm on land, instead out on the water.

This storm had to be bigger than the one that landed us here. The tunnel was great protection; I felt I was in a house, nice and safe. The storm continued into the night, we watched as we could still see the lightening in the distance and hear the thunder as the storm moved away, it continued to light up the sky, it was so bright, it looked like day light sometimes. We loved watching storms as long as we had cover. Frank walked back into the tunnel about twenty-five feet, and came back out and said "You can't hear anything in the tunnel, it is like nothing is going on outside. This is one weird place.

It was getting late, so we had to decide where we were going to settle down for the night. It really wasn't hard to decide, we went up to the theater room. We picked up our things and headed up the stairs, as we got closer to the room, it was getting warmer. The storm had brought the cold with it, and it was a little chilly in the tunnel, but once we were in the room, it was around 70 degrees. It felt good, to be warm again. We didn't have much clothes on, we normally don't, just a shirt, shorts and shoes when were not on the beach. We had the sleeping bags around us, as we watched the storm earlier.

I wanted to show Frank all the pictures and writings I had found, so for the rest of the evening we were looking at the walls in the theater room. He agreed it did look like it was telling a story about the history of the people that lived here. This has been another long day, I think we have been here on this part of the island for almost three weeks, time is lost here. Frank and I agreed tomorrow we will look at what he had found in the forest, I'm sure it will be nice and sunny again. The storms move pretty fast through the island, this time was a downpour. All the springs will be full of fresh water again. Well tomorrow is another day and Frank is already sleeping.

CHAPTER 19

WHEN I WOKE, I wasn't sure where I was, I reached for Frank, but he wasn't there. I sat up trying to find him, and then I yelled "Frank" I could hear him, he was in the hallway. About that time he came walking out "Morning sleepy head, I assume you slept well!"

I just smiled and stretched my arms out and said "Well yes I did, how about you?"

Great and I didn't wake up once, it is so quite in here, there was nothing to wake me up, and even your snoring didn't bother me!" Frank replied.

Frank had been looking at the writing on the walls, and he wanted to see if there was any by the color rooms, maybe they were labels on the rooms. He said "Each of them did have different writing. The yellow room had writing like this: ///_\\\, the red room ((*)), the blue room 8(*, (it wasn't an 8 but it kind of looked like one)."

If we had to guess, this is a temple of healing and closure. The people came here to see their favorite place one more time before they died. The color rooms are used to heal them; color healing had been used by Humans for a very long time. This is a lot like the Circle of Life, the way it heals the Merbeings.

From what we could figure out from the art work on the walls, these people came from the sky, and lived side by side with the Humans and Merbeings. They became one race in time, and raised their families here. The wall painting showed two large cities, one on top of a mountain range. We're assuming this is the mountain we're on and the one we found at the other end of the island.

According to the painting on the walls if we go out into the forest we will find many smaller villages and an area where they kept their animals.

As we walked around the room, we saw more pictures, there was Beings coming from the sky, but this time there was a war, and then sickness. Maybe, that was when they built this temple inside of the mountain. It is sad to think how it was from being a lovely, growing place to a war zone. We just stood there for a little while, and then Frank said "Let's pick up our gear and head out on our next discovery."

We gathered everything up, and took one last look before we headed down the stairs. I told Frank "We should come back here next year; it was nice to see the different places. Now that we know we can control the dream time."

Frank agreed "It would be a nice change; it would be like going on a vacation!

We got to the end of the tunnel and there was about a foot of water from the storm inside the hole, so we had to get wet. Frank went up first and then I would tie the gear up in the net and Frank would pull it up, then I went up. It was another beautiful day. We walked on to the beach, and there were piles of junk everywhere. I think the ocean decides to clean itself out.

I turned to Frank; I guess discovery is out today, we have work to do. We went ahead and put our gear up and headed to the first pile, there really wasn't much we could use, and the next four piles were the same. As we were walking down the beach we could see something moving. So we went to see what it was, as we got closer we could see there was five Dolphins, somehow they had gotten pushed on to the beach.

We went to work, pulling them by their tails, back into the water, as soon as they were close enough they would turn and head into the water. They called to the other ones on the land, Frank told them in Merbeing language "We'll get them, just stay there."

So they stayed back and waited. The last one wasn't looking to good, so we walked out into the water with her, and held her until she started moving better. Of course, the other four we're right there with us, it didn't take long before she started wiggling and started swimming on her own.

They all swam off together, and then turned and called back to us with a thank you. The four of them did some tricks for us, to show their appreciation for help. I guess the fifth one wasn't up to it. It is a great day, when you can save a life.

20

THE REST OF the day we were going from pile to pile seeing what we could use and what we can burn or bury. Any garbage that we cannot use our burn we felt it was better to bury it so it wouldn't go back out to the ocean again. We have dug a lot of holes since we've been here. As usual, there was lots of rope and nets to be had.

After spending a couple of days collecting ropes and nets we decided to make ourselves a couple of hammocks and a roof over our heads. It wasn't that hard to do! We layered the nets, so they would be solid, but yet comfortable hammocks, then we used the rope. By weaving the rope in between the netting holes, then tied each end to a tree. Of course before we started the roof we decided we needed to test out the hammocks. They were really comfortable; I'm looking forward to sleeping tonight!

But Frank as always, wanted to get all the work done before we relaxed, so we set off to do the roof. It's basically the same thing we did with the hammock but it had to be three times as big as the hammock. After we did all the weaving and connecting the ropes to the netting, we tied the ropes to different trees from the hammocks. This of course was a challenge because we had to get it high enough up, so we could get underneath it. Frank has gotten really good at climbing the trees. He would take each end up, secure it and then come back down the tree and go to the next one. After he tied the last rope, I handed up palm branches from the trees, this would help protect us from the rain. We normally, had rain about every three days, I guess that is why the island is so green, and has so many different types of plant life.

We completed our vacation home, if I do say so; this is a nice cozy place for us to stay now. We had built a fire pit earlier in the week. We could smoke some of the fish, so we could take them on our adventures.

After we tested the hammocks for a while we decided to take another walk down to the beach, and see how much farther it would be to the end of the island. Funny after all these years we still haven't made it to the other end of the island, there is always something to distract us from getting there. We could almost see the end, but the island turned again, we were not sure if it's just the tip of the island or if it goes on even farther.

This was no different than any other time! We walked to the shoreline so we could see how high the mountain was and if there was any path that we could take to get to the top. We did spot two different paths that looked like it might lead to the top of the mountain. Frank and I talked about heading up to the top to see what was there. We wanted to see if we could find the holes that were in the theater room and if there was any other entryway into the mountain.

Frank suggested that we catch a bunch of fish and smoke them for our trip up the mountain. You never know what we will see or end up doing! As we walked back to camp, I turned to him and said "We didn't make it to the end of the island again!" "Yeah I know" said Frank.

We headed back to camp to get the fishing poles, as we were walking back I spotted some fruits that we could use on our trip. Frank told me to go ahead and get the fruits and plants and he would go ahead and do the fishing. Which was great because I really hate fishing, Frank is definitely the hunter in our marriage.

The rest of the day and evening was getting things prepared for the trip up the mountain. We always like to prepare for three days of journey. It should only take a day, but we have learned to plan for anything.

We finally got everything done and climbed into our hammocks. What a wonderful feeling, they were the most comfortable thing we have slept in a long time. The beds that we have in the house by the bay, we put a lot more work into. Frank had made a wooden frame and then we filled it up with the leaves and dry grass. Every once in a while we would have to go out and get more leaves and grass and fill it back up again, kind of like changing your sheets or fluffing your pillows.

Sleeping on the ground was getting harder to do, so it is nice having the hammocks, and a covered shelter to sleep under. Granted we do have the tarp but it is getting pretty worn. When the wind blows it doesn't stop the rain from coming down on you. We removed the tarp on the shore side, and rolled it up. If a storm did come in, we would be ready for it this time.

21

WHEN WE GOT up the next morning, the smoked fish and plants that needed to be dried were ready to be packed up. I'm going to miss those hammocks; I haven't slept that good in weeks. I think Frank really slept well too, all I could hear was his snoring.

The path that we had seen yesterday was just around the corner, so we thought. We walked in and out of the forest trying to find the path for about an hour or so and then I found it. I yelled for Frank, and told him I had found the path, well I think I did.

Frank took the lead and I followed him up the mountain. It wasn't the easiest path we've been on. It looks like it hasn't been used in a long time but at one time there must've been steps going up the mountain here. We would find stones layered like steps for about ten feet and then they would disappear and there would be nothing but dirt again. So I guess we were on the right path. About halfway up the mountain we found a clearing, so we took a break. As we turned to look at the ocean, you could see all the way to the horizon and there was nothing, absolutely nothing to see except water. This is the highest we have been on the island;

we couldn't see the other side yet. But I'm pretty sure it's the same view.

After a break we started heading back up the mountain and we kept a lookout for the air holes from the theater room or any kind of opening that may access the rooms below. We didn't see any kind of entrance when we were inside of the mountain, but we didn't see the other staircase either.

Because of the terrain it took a lot longer than we thought it would, to climb the mountain. But we finally made it to the top! It was a view that was beyond belief, as far as you could see there was nothing but ocean except for the island we were on. We could see the Bay where we lived with the Roslanders; we could even see the outline of the city that is underwater on both sides of the island. As we looked over to the other side, it looked like there was another large bay at one time but now is underwater. This had to be one amazing city at one time! We decided that we would spend the night on top of the mountain and enjoy the view. There were no thunder clouds in the sky so we felt pretty safe that we wouldn't get caught in a storm.

As Frank and I cleared off an area to lay our sleeping bags down and have dinner, you could feel the cold breeze and the fresh smell of the ocean. After we finished eating we decided to look around and see if we could find anything else of interest. Frank went one direction and I went the other. When all of a sudden I heard a loud crash, and then I heard Frank screaming in pain. My heart jumped out of my chest as I ran towards where the last time I saw Frank. He had found another hole but this time he wasn't as lucky, he was just lying there, not moving. I yelled his name and he looked up at me, said a couple swearwords and then laid his head back down again. I asked him if he was okay and he said "No, I think I broke my arm!"

The hole wasn't too big or deep, about 3 feet deep and 4 foot wide. I have no clue what it could have been used for. I asked Frank if he could get up and he said "Not right now just let me sit here for a little while."

I sat on the edge of the wall waiting for him to let me know if I could help him or not. He didn't sound too good, so I told him he needs to get up and let me help him out of the hole. He finally agreed and started to get up.   First on his knees, than he tried to use his broken arm, he screamed and remembered it was broken. So once he was on his knees I was able to jump down into the hole to help him get up. Normally, it wouldn't have been a big deal getting out of the hole for Frank, but this time it was going to be a challenge for both of us.

We agreed I would go back and get the shovel and dig stairs of sorts so he could walk up the hole. So I climbed out of the hole, which wasn't easy but I did it. I ran to the campsite, and grabbed the shovel and some rope. You never leave home without your shove or rope! I ran back to the hole where Frank was still on his knees, I could tell he was in a lot of pain, but at least the bone wasn't sticking out of his arm.

It didn't take me long to dig steps into the side of the hole so he could get up and then I tied a rope around his chest and around the tree so I could help pull him up. This was to make sure that he doesn't fall back into the hole. It worked really well and once he got up to the top of the hole, he set back down again. I told him we need to get back to camp (on top of the mountain) and see what we can do about his arm. He agreed and got back up; swearing a little bit more and we headed back to the camp.

It was a good thing that we both knew first-aid and how to set a broken arm. By the looks of it he just cracked it, because I couldn't feel any broken bones under his skin. I went and got some tree limbs and cut them to fit his arm, and then I took some material and rope and tied it around his arm. I had to cinch it pretty tight to make sure he wouldn't use it. I know he wanted to scream bloody murder, but he held it in, because he didn't want me to get upset. Too late!

One good thing about learning about the plants on this island is I knew what plant to go find to give him, which would help with his pain. We'll have to stay here, on top of the mountain for a couple days. At least until he can get around a little bit better. There is no way he could climb down the mountain the way he is right now. Good thing we plan on a couple of days up here, and had enough supplies to last. Granted if I needed to, I could go back to camp and get whatever we may need. But I really don't what to leave him here.

I settled Frank in; I had him laying on both of the sleeping bags, and had piled rocks to hold his arm in place. Then I headed out to find the plants I needed. The plant I needed was all over the island, but for some reason there wasn't any on top of the mountain. I really hated letting Frank out of my site, but I needed to find the plants. He said he would be ok, and promised not to move. So I headed down the mountain, until I found the plants, it was the berries I needed not the plant itself. I gathered up a handful, being careful not to get the juice on my hands. If I did it would numb my hand in less than two minute.

Once I got back to Frank, I found a cup and a rock to smash the berries up. Then I took the juice and rubbed it on his arm and shoulder too. It will help kill the pain. It didn't take long before he started feeling better. This is great stuff, if only I knew what the plant was called.

Frank agreed with me and said "It feels much better; it doesn't hurt as much as before! I'm sure glad you took the time to learn about the plants on this island from the healer." I had learned the different things these plants can do for us and the Merbeings.

After a while Frank got up and told me to pull the sleeping bag from under him, so I would have something to sleep in. I did, better now than later when he started feeling the pain again. We settled in for the night, the sky was even brighter on top of the mountain than on the beach. If it wasn't for the moon, there wouldn't have been any light except the stars. It was an amazing view; it's too bad that Frank had to break his arm.

It was a long night; Frank couldn't get comfortable, he's not use to lying on his back to sleep. Needless to say the brace on his arm wasn't that easy to lay still with either, but it was better than nothing.

The berries only lasted about four hours and then I had to crush more up and reapply the juice to his arm and shoulder again. The next morning his arm didn't look too good, in the night it had started to swell and the brace was too tight on him. I had used all of the berry juice up during the night; I had to go get more berries to crush. I told Frank when I got back I would remove the brace and apply the berry juice on his arm again but it was going to hurt like crazy. It had to be done; otherwise he would have a lot more problems. I went off down the mountain to get the berries, and hurried back to him. He really wasn't looking too good; he had a fever and was sweating. I told him to hang in there and let me fix his brace.

As I removed the brace, I noticed there was something sticking in his arm, which I hadn't seen before. It was a thorn of some type, so I pulled it out and you could tell that it was causing problems. The area the thorn was in had already started accumulating pus and redness around it. I cleaned out the area and put some other plants I had from my kit to help with pulling the poison out. Then I put a band aid on it, to ensure that no dirt would get into it. Then I put the juice from the berries, that I had crushed up earlier and lathered his arm all the way up his shoulder. Not only does the berries numb the area that it is apply to, but it also can be used as a sedative as it absorbs into the skin. Once it started working, I put his brace back on. While I was doing that he fell back to sleep, or he passed out either way he'll get some rest.

It was hard to see Frank like this, but I'm sure he'll be okay after a couple days rest. I decided to wander around and see what I could find, but I made sure I stayed close enough so I could hear Frank, if he woke up and needed me. I wanted to see if I could find the plants that Frank had received the thorn from, so if he did get worse I could show the Merbeing healer and she could tell me what to do.

I walked over to where Frank had fallen into the hole earlier, to see if I could find the plant. As I got closer to the hole, I found the plant that had the thorns on it. Frank must have hit the plant when he fell into the hole. I still had the rope tied to the tree, which I used to get Frank out of the hole. I decided to climb down into the hole and see if I could tell what the hole was used for. It had rocks built around the inside of the hole; it looked like they had been stacked on top of each other. Maybe this was a well at one time, there were a few colored stones throughout the wall, and the stones looked like calcite, and were yellow, green and blue stones.

There wasn't much else to look at, but I did collect some of the calcite and quartz stones for healing purposes later. I climbed back up on the rope and got out of the hole. I untied the rope from the tree and rolled it up, to take back to camp with me. It was time to go check on Frank anyway. When I got back to Frank, he was still out and it looked like his fever had broken. I had covered him up with my sleeping bag before I left to make sure he didn't get a chill, but he had thrown it off in his sleep.

I needed to get some water and food into him, so I had to wake him up, which wasn't an easy task; he was really out of it.

Once I gave him food and water, he was ready to go back to sleep. I told him I wanted to check his wound and make sure that it was still clean. He grumbled then said "Okay!" When I put the bandage on his wound earlier, I made sure I wouldn't have to take off his brace again to clean it. He didn't need to go through that again! His wound looked pretty good, I needed to clean it out again, and it still had a little redness and pus. But I think it'll be fine now!

By the time that I had cleaned the wound and checked his brace, Frank was starting to wake up.

He asked me "What have you been up to?"

I told him that I went and checked out the hole and found the plant that had the thorns on it, so I got a sample for the healer to look at.

Frank replied "Good idea, the more we know about these plants the better off we will be!"

I gave him a little more water and told him to rest, I'm going to need to go down to the other camp and get us more water. I had used most of the water to clean his wound; as a result we were running out of water.

He didn't like the idea of me going down the mountain by myself (he's always so protective). I told him I would be fine and I will be very careful! Before I left I put more of the berry juice on his arm and shoulder to help with the pain. I figured it would knock him out and I would be back before he knew it. Mostly, because I knew he would be worried the whole time I was gone.

Once he fell asleep I headed down the mountain. It is much faster going down the mountain, than climbing up, that's for sure! It also was nice that we had made a path; it made it much easier to get down. Once I reached the beach, it felt so nice to be on a flat surface. I reached the camp, and started getting more supplies, band aids (which was just cloth we had found on the beach in the past) and more berries. There were a lot more berries here on the lower level of the island, than on top of the mountain. Then I headed out to get fresh water, I filled up the bottles. I sat down for the first time in awhile and drank my fill and then refilled the bottles again.

I spotted some plants we could eat, and thought it would be nice to have some fresh plants, with our dried fish for a change. Oh Ok, I'm ready to head back up the mountain! I just hope Frank was still sleeping, if he is doing better tomorrow, we'll head back down the mountain.

I took another break before I headed up the mountain; I knew it was going to take everything I had to get back up to Frank. Mostly, because I was carrying supplies and it has been a long day so far. As I sat there, looking out at the ocean, I had to wonder what would of happen to me if Frank wasn't here. Funny, I never really thought about it before, the good news is; he is here and I need to get going.

After taking a few breaks on the way up, I finally made it back to Frank. He was just sitting there and smiling at me. It was good to see him awake and smiling. I went over to him and gave him a kiss, and gave him some water.

I told him, "Your looking much better, how are you feeling?"

"Better, I had this great nurse keeping care of me, I wonder where she went?" Frank joked. I just laughed and replied "Funny"

I UNPACKED THE SUPPLIES, and made some lunch for us. Good old salad and dry fish coming up! It was good to see Frank eating, he said, "That berry juice really worked well, I think tomorrow, we can make a smaller brace. I think the break is in my lower arm."

I told him "I picked more berries while I was back at the other camp, so when we make the new brace we'll just put a smaller one on, otherwise you'll be knocked out again.

Frank said, "I what to see the hole I fell into and the stones you told me about."

Are you up to it, I don't want you over doing it, I told him.

He said, "I won't! But while we are up here, I want to check the mountain top out! As we stood at the top, we could see all direction. We both agreed this is a beautiful view. The ocean is so blue and the island is a lot bigger than I thought it would be!"

The water is so clear we can see to the bottom, on one side you can see the underwater city, it is huge, and sea life is everywhere, from fish to plants. Even from the distance you could tell there were all kinds of colors in the cities. From the fish and the large sea plants, they were moving in rhythm with the water, moving back and forth.

We finally could see the other end of the island. We walked to the edge, and it was a cliff that went straight down, there is no way we could get around it on foot. The water looked really deep; it was the darkest blue we have seen around the island. We'll have to ask Trido about it. We have wondered if there may be an entry way into the mountain. Nothing would surprise us at this point.

As we walk around we found stones stacked on top of each other, it looked like there may have been a wall here at one time. The wall started at the hole Frank had fallen into and the wall was a funny shape, it looked like it could have been a pyramid and the hole was at its top.

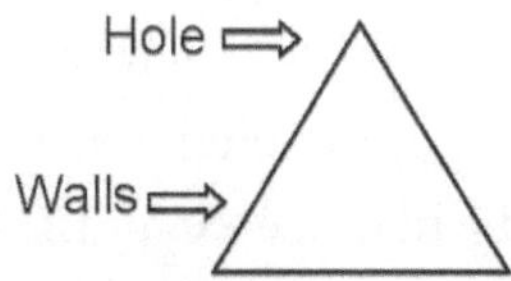

Just another weird thing! Right? Frank agreed, as we headed back to camp. Frank said, "I need to take a break and get some more plant juice on my arm."

I had used the last of the berry juice earlier. I told him I need to go get some more berries, just sit down and drink some water and I'll be right back. I headed down the mountain, when I saw something in the distance. I couldn't believe it, it was a plane. I yelled at Frank "Look, over there!" All he could say was "I'll be damned! I didn't think we would ever see one of them again." Granted it was too far away to see us, but at least we know there is still life out there. As far as we know, we could be the only two humans left on this planet. Well that was our excitement for the day. I headed down the mountain to find more berries; Frank went back and sat down at the camp.

After getting the berries ready and applied it to Franks arm, I looked at his wound; it looked like it was getting worse. I had to clean it out again and put another band aid on it. Frank settled in for a nap, so I lay next to him. It was nice, we were laying under a tree for the shade, and the breeze would come and go.

A couple hours later we woke up, hungry! I prepared some food and then Frank and I talked about what we had found. We needed to get off the mountain, before another storm arrived. We have been really lucky so far. He was feeling pretty good, so we decide to head down, if it became too much for him; there was a place for us to stop. The plant was doing its job and keeping Frank out of pain, I'm sure the nap helped too. We had to stop a couple of times, mostly because I had to carry most of the camping gear back down the mountain. Frank just smiled at me and said "Sorry, I should have been more careful." I agreed with him, and told him he needed to stop falling into holes! Then I gave him a kiss, and said its fine I can handle it! Once we hit the beach, I helped Frank remove his backpack and then I helped him sit down. It is funny how you don't realize, how much you use your arms, when you sit.

As we sat on the beach and drank some water, it was nice to just sit there and enjoy the sounds of the ocean. Once we were rested up, we headed back to the main camp; we would rest for a day and then head back home to the bay. The nice thing is, tonight we sleep in our hammocks, and have some fresh food for a change.

CHAPTER

 **23** 

WHAT A WONDERFUL night, had a great dinner, played some cards, and enjoyed the evening lying in our hammocks. One thing we both agreed on, were not going to be rescue from here. There is no land or any sign of human life to be seen. I really don't count the plane I saw; it could have been a bird. The only way we will ever get off this island is if we build us a boat. I don't see that happening either.

It was a little harder for Frank to get in to his hammock. I haven't laughed so hard in a long time, watching him trying to get into the hammock. Well he did say he didn't need any help but after awhile I helped him get into it.

I stood on the other side of the hammock and held it for him, and he just sat down into it, and put his legs up. I helped pull his sleeping bag up to his chest. I had put the plant juice on his arm earlier in the evening so he wasn't in too much pain. I also think that is why I won all of the card games!

Frank was up before me the next morning, he had went out and picked some berries for his arm. He told me "I tried to go fishing, but I just couldn't do it. I just can't cast with my left hand. You will to have to do it, as he smiled"

Something I should tell you I stink at fishing, I have lost a few poles in my time. But to make it even worse, when I do put the line in the water, the fish take off in the other direction. I swear this to be true!

I told Frank "How do you feel about clams and the sea urchin to eat?" He agreed, but only if I would try fishing for thirty minutes, if you don't catch anything, I'll help with the clams and urchin! Agreed? Agreed!

We headed out to the shore line and he pointed at where I should cast my line. I just laughed, yea like I could do that. But I tried it and sure enough I caught something, it was Frank! He swore a little, and pulled the hook out of his shirt and told me to try again. This time he moved away from me. So I tried it again, and this time the line went out into the water. He yelled "Good job, now just bring it in slowly." I followed his instruction, and the next thing you know, the fishing pole left my hand. I heard Frank in the back ground, "Get it!"

SO I dived for the pole and caught it before it took off into the ocean. I started running back to the shore with my pole in hand and Frank yelled "Stop, turn around and bring it in slowly."

To my surprise, I caught a fish, a nice size one too! Frank was telling me "Great job." He said it was the funniest thing he had seen in awhile. I was soaking wet, but I still had my pole and fish! I guess we both had a good laugh, in the last 24 hours. Then he told me, "You're going to have to clean it too!"

Here's the thing I also hate cleaning fish, I can never get it right, half the meat is full of bones and the other side has hardly any meat on it. Let alone it is just icky! But it is just another thing I'll have to do. I'm beginning to think Frank broke his arm on purposes. Not really!

The fish didn't turn out to bad, I made fish soup and set the rest to being smoked. It was time to change Frank's band aid and clean his wound. Both are looking much better, we agreed that he didn't need his brace anymore, but I would just wrap his arm and only use one stick, instead of the three. His wound was almost gone, his arm still hurt but he didn't want to put anymore juice on it. He didn't like the way it knocked him out every time.

After I played nurse, we decided to go for a walk in the forest; needless to say we were looking out for holes. I was in front this time and I had a stick that I would poke the ground in front of me. Frank was behind me, laughing, and said "It's going to take forever to get anywhere this way!" Better safe, then have a broken arm! I replied back. All he could say was "True!" As I poked the ground in front of me, to make sure there wasn't any holes to fall into.

We found another building; it wasn't that big, maybe a 14 x 14 feet, compared to the other buildings we had found. It had two opening, and it looked like it had a few windows. Of course, all of these building we have seen, have no roof and the walls are not that high, but there was enough to see what it might of looked like at one time. There was nothing inside the building, accept for plants and trees. Also, some of the wild life had made parts of the building their home.

The forest on this side of the island was a little different than the Bayside where we lived. This side had what seemed to be roads, and would enter an area that was flat and had flat stones underneath the dirt. If I had to guess it would be the city center and the roads all led to it. The forest on the island had different trees on each end of the island. This side has a lot more palm trees and other tropical plants. On the side where we live, there are different types of trees and plants. I really wouldn't know what type of trees they are, some looked like maple trees. They make great shade trees! There are a lot of herbal plants that can be used for healing, throughout the island.

We spent the day just looking around and looking at the different plants. Any plants that we hadn't seen before, we would take a sample to show the healer when we got back to the bay.

It is amazing to see a city that once was a thriving city at one time, and nothing left except the buildings to tell a story. We found a few more buildings and an area that must've been used for animals. The reason I say this is, there was feeding troughs and fencing of sorts, and we could see fence post sticking out of the ground.

We decided to have chicken tonight for dinner, the problem was I would have to catch and kill it. Another thing I normally didn't have to do. Catching it wasn't too hard; Frank had a sure way of catching them. He would use one of our nets and tie it to a couple of trees, and then he would chase the chickens into the net and then pulled the net on top of them.   Chasing the chicken around in the forest is not an easy task. Frank really couldn't chase anything because of his arm, but he would stand there and yell at the chicken if it came his way. After about thirty minutes, I finally got the chicken to go into the net. First step done! Frank said he would kill the chicken for me; at least he could do that much for me, after having me running around the forest, chasing chickens.

I won't go into details about how he kills the chickens, but it was all worth it! The chicken was a nice change from the seafood. We roasted the chicken and then I made a soup out of the leftover meat. We found that it was better to make the leftovers into soup, which we can put in a container for later. As we settled in for another night, we talked about all the different things that we have seen in the last couple of weeks. We can only use our imagination of what the city was like many years ago. We settled in for the night, as we wondered what was going to happen tomorrow.

24

AFTER ANOTHER GREAT night in our hammocks, it was time to pack up and go home, back to the bay. We walked until we arrived at the rock formation that blocked our way. We had to wait for the tide to go out the next day. We tired up the hammocks and settled in for another night out.

The tide went out early morning, so we were up before the sun came up, and we packed up our things and headed around the rocks. Once we got to the other side of the rocks we saw there were all kinds of things on the beach, left over from the storm earlier. I turned to Frank and said we'll clean up the beach later! He agreed, but it didn't stop us from looking at the different piles as we walked by them.

There was couple of things we picked up, one thing was a bike wheel, and Frank already had plans for it use. There were some glass floater; we thought we would pick them up for Esaw and Trigut. I wanted to keep one of them for myself, the colors were beautiful. These were not from a fishing boat, but made to look at or hang up somewhere. Esaw and Trigut will enjoy them.

Then we saw this box, we love it when boxes come ashore! We never knew what we will find. As we opened it we could smell something from the past, it was fruit! Oranges, apples and melons, and was all still good, by the looks of it. I couldn't help it; I grabbed an apple and bit into it. Oh my god, I couldn't believe the flavor, it was wonderful. With my mouth full, all I could say to Frank was "It's great!" Frank grabbed one, and we both stood there with our mouth full of apple, making yummy sounds and smiling at each other, like kids with candy for the first time. After we finished the apple, we went for an orange; we ate it with the peel and everything. Again, "It was wonderful, we really missed fruit. There is fruit on the island, bananas, coconuts and other types of fruit; I don't know what to call them. Anyway, I can't wait to try the melons!

We agreed to wait until we got back home, to eat some more. We loaded it up on our cart, which Frank made with the bicycle wheel, tree branches and rope. That man can build anything! It was much easier than dragging it behind us.

We continued on our way home, checking out the other piles, we will need to come back; there must have been a flood somewhere. The things we were seeing came from homes not from a ship. It is sad, but their loss is our gain! Hope everyone was ok!

We didn't have far to go, and I could tell Frank's arm was starting to hurt, so I told him I needed to take one more break before we finish our trip. He didn't say anything he just pulled the box from the pile, and said "Have a sit, how about another apple?" I smiled and opened the box and grabbed two apples for us. As we sat on the box, and watched the ocean rolling in the sun light, but in the distance we could see thunder clouds coming our way. We still had plenty of time to get home. We watched the clouds and saw the lighting inside the clouds. I told Frank "Good thing were not on top of the mountain, all we need to happen, is get hit by lightening!"

We finished our apples and started to head home, this time I took one side of the wagon. Frank protested for a little bit, until I gave him "the look" and then he just moved over. Next stop home!

We arrived at our home by the forest; nothing had change there, except the storm had done a little damage to our house by the bay. It looked like the water came up farther than normal, but we didn't have anything in it anyway. We'll just have to put it back together again!

The bed was calling to us, so we put the fruit in the shade, and jumped into bed. It was so nice to move around, without worrying about falling out. Don't get me wrong, I loved our hammocks, but our bed at home was amazing!

After our nap, Frank started working on a way to keep the fruit fresh longer; his arm was almost like new. I had used the healing stone on it earlier, and used some herb we had at the house. Natural healing is the best!

He dug a hole and put the stones into a square, they came from the ancient city. He put the little cooler in the hole, we found it on the beach earlier, and it didn't have a top. I made one out of bamboo and plant slime, when it dried it was as hard as rock. Once it did dry, we tested it to make sure it would work. It did, so Frank put the fruit inside the cooler box, and then put the top on it.

He told me "It will keep it fresh, but it will also stop bugs from getting to the fruit. I was telling him how smart he was, and he told me "I got it out of the book from Gary Dean "How to fix things." I just used the stones, instead of wood and the cooler instead of insulation. I told him it works, that's all I care about.

But I asked, why did you put the rocks in the hole, without even thinking twice Frank said "You're going to want to clean it once and awhile Right? This way we won't have to dig out the hole each time!"

How could you argue with that!

We hadn't had pork in a while, so Frank went hunting. We tried not to eat too much pork when the Roslanders are here, because they don't like the smell of it cooking. Frank came back with a nice size one, and he had already cleaned it. It was ready for the fire pit. I put my herbs and other plants inside of it. Tonight we have pork, salad and melon for dinner! Life is good!

CHAPTER

25

TODAY WE ARE just doing recovery (this is a military term, for cleaning and putting things up); we hung the hammocks up and put the ropes and nets up too. I hung my glass ball up on a stick outside our house. I can see it through the window; it is beautiful when the sun hits it.

After we squared everything away, we went down to the bay and worked on the bay house, and then we took a break. We had left-over's from dinner; and the cooler that Frank made is working out great.

After lunch, we went back to the bay and hung out there for awhile. We were wondering when the Roslanders would be back. Tride and Trigut should have had their second child by now! It'll be great to see all of the Roslanders again. I'm sure they will have stories to tell us, and do we have stories to tell them!

The next couple of days we were cleaning up the beach, and seeing if there was anything else we could use. We moved most of the wood up to the house, for cooking and smoking our food. Frank had made a smoking hut awhile ago; it was big enough to put a couple of fish or a couple of chickens in it. We normally cooked the pig over an open fire.

Next on our list was to make small nets for the Roslanders to use for their fishing, and bigger ones to hold the fish in the bay. Most of the nets we get from the ocean are damage. We have to repair them, usually we will put two nets together to cover all of the holes, and then use the rope to tie them together. We pull the big ropes apart, so there are six small ones, and then use them to do the repairs or tie the nets together. We added a loop so the Roslanders can use their spears to throw the nets even farther, and a smaller rope with about seven feet length, so they can just pull it back to them. We don't do the length of rope on all of them; it's more for fun, than anything else. It's kind of like roping cattle! It works great for Frank, when he is fishing with the Roslanders!

Well the last few weeks, we have been hard at work, cleaning, fixing and gathering. The beach looks as good as new, and all of the repairs have been done. It's time to go exploring; we are going to check out our ancient city. The earth quake from earlier this year, had opened up some new areas, we have wanted to check out.

According to the moon, it will be only a couple of weeks before our friends will be back. At least this time we won't have to pack up supplies to go exploring. We just grabbed some ropes and water and headed into the forest, it didn't take long before we were at the ancient city. I think this city was in better shape than the one on the other side. I wonder what the cities names were.

There were two new holes, and we went to the first one and lowered a flashlight down the hole, to see if we could see anything. It lit up a big room, for a little bit and then it went out. I guess the battery finally died. That told us it was safe to go down, there wasn't any water in the hole and it was big enough for us to go in. Off we go!

CHAPTER

26

I T WAS OUR normal process; we tied our rope ladder to a couple of trees and threw it down the hole. It was much easier to go up and down the rope ladder than just using a rope. I wish we would have taken it with us on our last adventure, but we didn't think we would need it. Boy, we were wrong!

Once we got down to the bottom, we turned on our flashlight, (yes, after almost five years our flashlight worked, we had lots of batteries on our boat.) Anyway, as we were looking around there were all kinds of things, we couldn't see what it was. But as we shined our flashlight around, we kept hitting something that would reflect the light. I walked over to one; it was a clear quartz stone, about eight inches high. I cleaned it off and it started to glow, I went to the next one and did the same thing. Then Frank got the idea and started doing the same thing. Next thing that happened they started reflecting the sun light from the hole in the ceiling. The whole room was as bright as it was outside, it was remarkable. As we looked around we saw what the room was, it was a museum! It had artifacts displaying the way you would see them at a museum.

The room was much bigger than we first thought. It was attached to another room, which had minerals of great beauty, and power! When we walked into the room, we could feel the energy, much like we could feel from the Circle of Life.

The next room had mummies in it, there were five of them. Each a little different, there was one of a Merbeing, and the others were of humans and one we think was a green one. They must have been someone important; they were enclosed in a glass box, with some of their possessions. Each of them had writing on them, the writing was different but from what I could understand these were the peace makers of their time. The five bought peace to their cities and all Beings on the plant. It didn't matter what species or race you came from.

On the walls it had drawings of their history, like the theater room. I think the history was earlier though. Where the writing ended in this room, it began again in the theater room. How I wish we could show the world how it once was. As we were looking around, we could tell the holes were letting the weather in, some of the art work was damage.

Frank said "When we're done checking this out we need to fix the holes and seal it back up again, to protect it from anymore damage. I agreed, "We can use the bamboo and plant juice we used for sealing things, there's no way the weather will get in! There must be an entry way to this level. Frank agreed, we continued to look around and clean the quartz off as we went. It was really cool the way they glowed and pulled the light from one another. They were laid out in the right direction for the sun to go from one to the other. I wanted to see if I moved the stone, what would happen; it changed the direction of the light. I moved it back and it lit up the room again. Kind of like a light switch!

Each room was another section of history, we tried to draw some of what we seen, but we couldn't do it justice. So we gave up and continued to look around. If this museum was ever shown to the world, everything in history books would have to change.

After walking through six different rooms, we found the stairs; we also found the other hole we saw from the top. Frank turned to me and said "We have a lot of work ahead of us." I just smiled and said "Yeah, but protecting all of this is worth it. We walked up the stairs, but we couldn't get the door open, so we had to go back up the rope ladder. We had our measuring rope with us, so we measure how far it was to the stairway and then went to the top; we measured to find the steps and door on top.

After we tried a couple of times to find the door, we finally found the door. It had a big rock in front of it, as if to block it. We would of never known it was there, if it wasn't for the holes in the ground. We decided to head back to the bay and have dinner and enjoy the evening. Of course, we talked about what we had found, and how interesting the different rooms were. I asked Frank, what was your favorite room?

He said "The mummy of course, and what about you?" I said the mineral room! I have always loved minerals and stones; I had a large collection of them in Texas, but nothing like we saw today. It was incredible the stones that were in the room. The colors were beyond belief, and some of them were so big!

Franks asked me, "Did you see the skulls on the mummies, each was formed different. I don't know much about skulls, but I'm pretty sure some of them were not normal. There was writing below the names for them, but I couldn't read it. The writing looked a lot like the writing we found at the other end of the island.

The other things that we had discovered earlier, was a hole by the waterfall we used for our water supply. In the beginning we just walked around it, we just figured it was just another hole in the rocks. We were chasing a chicken for dinner when we discovered underneath the hole was another hole. The only reason we found it was because the chicken ran into the hole, to hide from us. The first thing that came to mind this could be a nice chicken coop. But Frank started pulling at the plants on the wall and removing them. The more we cleared the wall off; it became apparent it was a stone wall. We forgot all about the chicken.

I climbed up to the top of the rock, and sure enough the hole was inside the rock. Once we cleared everything away, it looked like a bathtub, and underneath was where you would build a fire. It took three days to get it all cleaned out. We agreed it was a bathtub. Either that or a really big cooking pot! It had two round holes inside the tub, one at one end and the other was at the bottom, in the middle of the tub. I would think that is how they drain it.

It even had its own way to fill it up. We found a man made ditch, it was lined with flat stone, on the bottom and both sides. It leads up to the waterfall. It had a stone at the end of the ditch to stop the water from coming down into the tub. When you removed the flat stone the water would flow down to the bathtub. Once the tub was full you just put the flat stone back to block the water. Then if you wanted a hot tub, all you had to do is build a fire underneath it, in the hole where we found the chicken in. It warmed the water enough to have a nice warm bath.

It was way too much work to keep the fire going and enjoy a bath at the same time. I'm sure it was great if you had someone else doing all the work. But it is nice when we just want to clean the salt water off us. After awhile the salt water would dry our skin out, so between the waterfall and bathtub we could get it washed off pretty good. Koro also told us about a plant that would help with our dry skin.

27

WE STARTED THE day by cutting down eight small palm trees, which isn't an easy task, all we had was a little hand ax. After we removed all the braches and cleared around the two holes, which were made by the earthquake a few months ago. We laid down the logs around the holes. Then we started cutting the bamboo, and tied them together. While Frank was connecting the bamboo together, I picked the plants we needed to make the sealer. I used some of the plants from the water too. When the two are mixed together it acts like sealer.

We closed one hole and then we went inside to see if there were any places it might leak. I went back up and filled in the holes we saw. Frank would let me know if it was filled or not. We did the second hole, but we had to leave enough room for Frank to go down and check for any light coming from the hole. We did the same process, except we put a door in; it didn't make sense to just close it up. I am sure we will want to go back down later. There is so much history and things for us to learn. It was like having our own private museum.

After three days of non-stop working, we completed the task, and it was just in time. Here comes another storm! It didn't look so bad, but you never know about these topical storms. One minute, it's just a little rain and wind, next it is a full force storm. We decided to go hang out in our house and wait for it to pass over.

This is the storming season, the weather can be beautiful one minute and the next the wind and rain will come in, and then it's gone. The thunder storms are something to watch, the whole sky and ocean just light up and it looks like they are playing tag with each other. It's the best show in town!

But tonight it was just a little rain, and wind. After it passed we went and sat out in front of our house. The air is so clean and the sky is so clear you can see every star in the universe. We just sat there and listened to the waves come in and in the distance you could hear the whales talking to each other.

The next thing we knew it was early morning; it still gets a little chilly in the morning here. I woke Frank up, he looked a little confused and then he woke up enough, to know what happened. I told him, let's go into the house, where it is warmer, he agreed and headed into the house. He almost missed the door, but I pushed him over, so he wouldn't hit the door frame. I guess he wasn't awake.

We woke to sounds coming from the bay; we got up and headed to the door to see what was going on. The Roslanders were back and Tride and Tridax was yelling and making noise to get our attention. We waved at them, and yelled we'll be down after we eat. They waved back and smiled, as they swam off to be with the rest of the family. We're glad to see they are back! But, they are back early, I wonder why!

After eating and cleaning up, we headed down to the bay. It was so good to see them all, almost the whole family was back except for Trigut, and she must still be in Utopia with her baby. We walked into the water and hugs all around, hugs are one thing that we all do. We were surprised the first time we saw Trido and Esaw hugging. They have seen Frank and I hug many times, in time we started hugging each other. Isn't that what families do?

Everyone was talking at the same time, the first thing I asked Tride is what Trigut had, and he said "A girl, she is beautiful, Of course!"

I told him "We wish we could see her."

Tridax spoke up "You can, just connect in with us!"

Your right, I guess we will have to later, how do you like your new sister? I asked.

"She doesn't talk, or anything else right now, but she does smile at me and likes to hold my finger. I guess she ok!" Tridax replied.

I noticed that Esaw's mother wasn't there, so I asked Esaw where her mother was, she replied, "She is staying with Trigut, to help with the baby in Utopia."

They asked us what we had been up to. Frank replied "We have been pretty busy. We went to the other end of the island, went inside the mountain, went to the top of the mountain, and broke my arm. Found fruit on the beach, and to top it off, we found a museum in the ancient city on this side of the island."

Trido replied "How's your arm?" He didn't act surprised what we had found and did all these other things.

Frank replied "Good, it hurts once and awhile, but Aggie put some herbs on it, so it's healing nicely."

I turned to Esaw and said "Men!" She just smiled and said "Yea, their all the same!"

28

WE HAD A great time visiting with the Roslanders, and as always had a feast with all of the Clan members. Esaw had brought new plants for us to try; she told us the Sanderlands had brought the plants from their island. They had a wonderful taste to them, kind of sweet and sour favor. She also brought back my favorite clams from their city under the sea, "Utopia." (Utopia is where they live underwater, when they are not here on Rosland).

I asked Esaw how are the Sanderlander Clan doing, have they moved back home yet?

She said, "Yes, they left the same time we did, for their home. The humans that was doing all the testing from their boats, left about a month ago. They wanted to make sure the humans weren't planning on returning. The scout said, "The humans took all of their equipment with them, this time, so hopefully they won't be back."

I agree it's hard to believe they are testing sound waves underwater. Too bad they don't know it is hurting all of the sea life in that area. Who knows, maybe they figured it out, I hope so!"

Frank had asked Trido how the PaImJa clans were doing. Trido told us that they have everything under control and everyone is getting along much better. After the "change" it took a little while for the Pagon and Imdom to learn to treat each other as equal. The Jamicaer Clan had been a big help, in keeping the peace between the two clans.

The Clans have been doing a lot of work on their island too, getting it prepared for this season. They needed to clear some of the junk that was in the bay, and to set up more tanning stones. It looked like there were Humans there at one time. We found statues and other items in the water; it must have been a city at one time. Much like our city here, in Rosland. Some of the clan members had already left, to get everything ready for the new comers. This will be the first time for many of the Pagon and Imdom, to live on an island and sunbathe. The ones that were with us on our last trip from the Pagon old city couldn't stop talking about how wonderful it was. The feeling of heat going into their bodies, it was like being reborn. Although, they did say, jumping into the water after sun bathing wasn't that much fun. It was quite a shock for them, to hit the cold water, after being so warm. But they did learn to go slowly into the water, instead of just jumping in. Others enjoyed the shock; they received when they jumped from hot to cold.

Then I asked Trido, did they find anything else in the cavern that Taim had discovered earlier? Trido reply "Funny you should ask when they followed the cavern all the way to the other end, it opened up on to another large cavern above water, much like the cavern we use here for our protection. It also had all kinds of Human items and remains in it. The remains were in holes inside the walls, high enough up so the water couldn't get to them. We are assuming that is what they were for, because we couldn't get up that high.

The Jamicaer Clan still go back to their island, I think they like having a break from the Pagon and Imdom, Trido smiled as he said this. He went on to tell us, that they did find a few things inside the cavern that we may be interested in. As soon as they get time to check it out, they will let us know what they have. Than Trido changed the subject, and asked what were you telling us about the other end of the island?

Frank and I looked at each other, wondering what that was about. I started telling them about our adventures, how Frank had fallen into a hole in the forest, and that is how we found the tunnel, that lead to the building Inside the mountain. Frank and I took turns talking about everything we found inside and about the dream and healing rooms.

Esaw asked us questions about the rooms, and how it felt and so on. Trido was more interested in how it was built. Frank told him, as far as I could tell it was built out of one big rock. There were no signs of cutting or lines, everything was smooth. The guys continue to talk about how they think the building was made.

Then after awhile we started talking about the top of the mountain and how Frank broke his arm. When I told them about the thorn, Esaw asked if I brought a sample back, I smiled and said, Of course! I told her I would bring down the plants tomorrow, so we can talk about them. I told her the plant the healer had shown me, worked really well. I also told her about how I used the berries from the plant you call Hanri. It put Frank out and did a great job of keeping the pain down.

After awhile Frank asked Trido, if he knew anything about the dark blue water at the end of the island. Trido said "A little, we don't go to that side of the island very much. There are always weird things going on in the water there. The water is very deep there, and I really don't know how to explain it, but the water gets light, it is hard for us to swim in it. For the first ten feet and then fifteen feet, it was all fine, then it was hard for us to stay up right, it was like we were floating."

Then Trido asked Frank, did you see how straight the cliff side was, it looks like something just cut the whole end of the island off. Frank told him, "I didn't get a good look at it; I guess we'll have to go back and check it out."

It was getting late so we said our good nights and headed up to the house. We played a couple of hands of cards, and then we went to bed.

29

THE NEXT MORNING we headed down to the bay, I was going to meet Esaw and the Healer Koro there. Frank was going to go swimming with Trido, Tride and Tridax, outside of the bay today. I was excited to show Esaw and Koro the plants, I had discovered on the other end of the island.

As Frank headed out into the water he was met by the three of them, Trido, Tride and Tridax. Frank had brought the raft so he could get out farther into the water. I sat on the stone on the jetty and waited for Esaw and Koro to show up, it didn't take long. To my delight some of the plants, they had never seen before, it was nice for a change to show them something they haven't seen. Koro was very cautious in touching the plants. She told me that just because I didn't have a reaction didn't mean that the Merbeings couldn't, which made sense to me. We spent the morning going through the plants and talking about what I had used some of them for and trying to figure out what we could use the other plants for. Koro said she would like to take them to the city under water and do some tests on them. I agreed and told her I was looking forward to hearing about what she discovers. All of the plants were in containers, so she could take them to her city.

She went on her way and took the plants I had given her so she could investigate them. Esaw and I visited for a while, when she asked if I would like to connect and see her new granddaughter. All I said was of course! We connected and I got to see the new baby. She was so cute, and of course she had hair on her head, it was kind of reddish and she had the biggest blue eyes you could imagine. She was about 2 ½ feet long at this point, for my calculation she was about six months old. In human standards she looks like she was about two years old. It was great to finally see her! Trigut and the new baby Trien should be back to the Rosland in a couple months.

Afterwards, Esaw wanted to hear about the museum we had discovered in the ancient city. I was so happy she asked I have been dying to talk about what we had discovered in the museum.

I described what had happened, that the earthquake had opened up a couple holes in the ground, which was the ceiling of the museum, and this is how we were able to discover the museum. When we first went down into the hole, we couldn't believe what we had found. There are six rooms, each has different exhibits, and one of the most interesting things was the mummies that we found.

I told her there were five mummies, each a little different, there was one of a Merbeing, and the others were of humans and one we think was a green one. We think they must have been someone important; they were enclosed in a glass box, with some of their possessions. At the end of each of the glass boxes there was writing on them. From what I could understand these were the peace maker of their time. The five bought peace to their cities and all Beings on the planet.

Esaw seemed to be very interested in them, as I described each of them in more detail; she told me that she had heard of these five Beings before. Her mother had told her story about how there was five great leaders, that lived on top of a mountain. There was one from each human life form. All the large problems or changes would go thought this counsel. Then the planet started to move the land, that the mountain was on, most of the land went into the waters and all that was left was an island. After everything you and Frank found, I think this is the island. That would explain a lot, we couldn't investigate the island the way you did. It is a good thing you and Frank came here. Otherwise, we wouldn't have never known about the things that you found!"

This would explain the theater room, the walls in side of the room were covered in art, and it looked like it was showing the history of this land. It didn't make sense before because it showed a landmass, instead of an island. But if the landmass sunk into the ocean, then it would make perfectly good sense. I can't wait until Frank comes back so I can tell him what Esaw has told me.

About that time Frank was coming back into the bay on the raft. He was by himself, I guess the guys went home; Esaw had left a little while ago. When Frank came ashore he had dinner, he had calms in one hand, and something behind his back and a big smile on his face. I knew that look; he had something in his hand, behind his back. I got up and started backing up; I never knew what he was up to, so I wanted to be ready. As he pulled his hand around front, I saw what he had. It was a huge lobster, and it didn't look to happy. I guess it knew who was going to be dinner tonight! This is one time; I'm going to miss not having any butter! We do have plants that taste and smell like garlic.

As Frank came over to me, he said, "There was a long line of them, so I just picked one up, and here he is." Trido said "They migrate through here each year, but this year they came a lot closer to the island, than normal."

Lucky for us, not so much for them, I guess the Roslanders picked up a few dozen of them too. There will be a feast tonight.

We can have some of our fruit with it. I went and got a pot big enough for the lobster to fit in, and started the water going.

Frank went and laid out in the sun to dry off and warm up, the water is warm here, but after awhile it does get to us humans! After we had our wonderful lobster and fruit salad, we went for a walk to enjoy the beautiful evening, just another day in paradise!

30

I GUESS FRANK AND Trido have been talking about the dark water at the end of the island and they wanted to go check it out. Frank had asked me last night if I wanted to go. Amusing question, as if he could leave me behind!

The plan was to take the raft to the other end of the island; the guys (Trido, Tride and Tridax) would pull us over there, just to save time. We would be back tonight; we only packed water and ropes. The food we would just catch or pick as needed.

We headed over to the bay first thing in the morning; the raft was already in the bay. We loaded it up and saw the guys waiting for us by the entry to the bay. Once we were outside the bay, they grabbed our rope and started pulling us. The only way to travel! A couple of younger Roslanders joined us; they wanted to see what the dark blue water was all about. Trido, because he is the King, he always had two scouts and two hunters with him, any time that he left the safety of the bay. We ended up having rather a large group going with us.

It didn't take long for us to get to the other end of the Island. We went around to the end and it did look like the whole end of the island was just cut off, it looked smooth. The only time we have ever seen a cut like that on a side of a mountain, is when humans cut into a mountain to build a road on land.

Trido and Frank had already talked about how to use the rope, to go into the hole. The scouts would go down first, and see how deep they could go before the water became buoy. Tridax wanted to go, but Frank told him, he needed him there, just in case we need to pull them back up. Frank was already in the water, so Tridax swam over to him and waited.

I sat in the raft, with the rope tied on to it, and we all waited. The rope we were using we had marked off every five feet awhile ago, this is what we used when we went exploring. They went the first ten feet with no problems, then fifteen, when they reach twenty feet, something happened. In just a few seconds, the rope started going faster; we grabbed the line, and stopped it. Then we started pulling the lines up, and when they were at fifteen feet again, the line became loose, and a couple of minute later, the scouts pop their heads up.

We could tell by their faces, something had happened. They both swam over to us and said "It was the weirdest thing, we had no problem, then all of a sudden, there wasn't any buoyancy in the water, and we just started sinking. It happened so quick, it was a good thing we had the ropes on us. Otherwise, we don't know how far we would have fallen."

Trido asked his scouts, "Did they see anything," and their reply to him, "It looked like there was a cave about the time that we started sinking. We didn't get a very good look into it, but we can go back down and try it again now that we know what will happen.

Curiosity was getting the better of the guys, after talking about what had happened they had decided to add more rope to their line, just in case the scouts needed it. Plus they wanted to move closer to the end of the island and use the wall of the island, instead, of going straight down into the dark water hole.

Hopefully this would help them reach the cave that they had seen earlier.

There was a little cove at the end of the island that we moved the raft onto, because the water was crashing into the cliff. We were afraid that the raft would get thrown against the rocks, and destroy it. We connected the ropes to the other ropes to make them longer. Then we were ready to have the scouts go back down into the dark water. But this time one of the hunters wanted to go with them to make sure that everything was safe. It was agreed it was the right thing to do!

As they started to swim down into the waters, we fed the ropes to them when they hit 15 feet it did the same thing, so we assume that they were in the dark water. We anxiously waited for them to pull on the rope and let us know that they were okay. After about 10 minutes the rope was pulled, hopefully it was them letting us know they were okay.

In the meantime, the rest of the Merbeings that were with us swam around the deep water and stayed outside of the dark water circle. They were watching the scouts and the hunter, from a distance, to ensure that they were okay. Pretty soon Tride came up to the top of the water and waved at us and yelled they were okay their inside of the hole in the mountain. Then he dived back down to watch them.

All Frank and I could do is sit, watch and wait to see what happened next. It seemed like forever, but it was about thirty minutes when the Merbeings came up to the surface again. Trido and Tride swam over to us. They told us that the scouts and the hunter were on the way back up. It looked like they had something in their hands, but they couldn't tell what it was, from where they were watching from.

A couple minutes later the scouts and the hunter surfaced. They did have something in their hand, but we couldn't tell what it was yet. As they swam towards us we walked down to the shoreline to meet them. As they got closer we walked into the water to join the rest of the Merbeings to look at what they had discovered. They handed the object to Trido, and we walked over to him to look at the object with them.

Trido handed it to me, and said "It is a pot, and it is made of gold! Look where I scratched it, it looks like there may be some writing on it." I was surprise that it was so heavy, and the markings on it are very unique. But the pod itself was really different to; it had a round bottom but had a long neck that was added at an angle. If I had to guess I would say a 45° angle, the neck was about an inch at the end of it. Because it looked like a drinking vessel of some type, but I'm not sure what it would have been used for. Especially, since it was made out of gold!

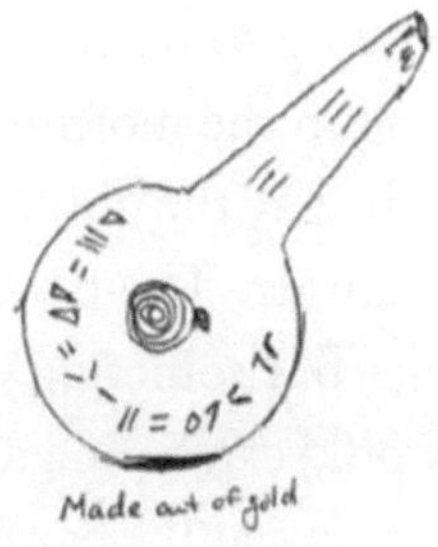

Made out of gold

The Scouts continued to tell us about what they had discovered, "This is all we could find. The cave had the reminiscent of at entry way at the far end of it, which looked like it went into the island but was blocked off many years ago. There was a ledge all the way around the cave; it was big enough for us to move along it. Otherwise, we couldn't have done anything. There was no water; it was an air pocket inside the cave and the surrounding water was part of the air pocket. It just was one big air pocket! We have never seen anything like this before."

The scouts and the hunter continued to talk about how weird it was inside the air pocket. The bottom of it was lined up with the cave, but yet there were no dead animals on the floor of the air pocket. They figured there should have been dead animals, because once you get into the pocket, you fall to the bottom like they would have done, if they didn't have the ropes on them.

Of course this got Frank and Trido, curious about what would happen if Frank went into the air pocket! So they started planning on how they were going to get Frank into the air pocket. It was only 10 to 15 feet until he would reach the pocket. So they figured they would use the diving gear to get to the air pocket and then he could remove it. After a while they came up with plan. But it was getting late so we all decided it was time to head home. We loaded up the raft and pushed it out far enough so the Merbeings could pull us back to the bay. We needed to get more equipment anyway and if we were going to do this we needed to be rested and ready to go first thing in the morning.

On the way back to the bay the hunters caught a few fish and a couple of octopus for dinner. The bay fish are normally what they would eat for dinner but sometimes other fish came along the shoreline that they would catch for a different taste. Esaw was waiting for us when we arrived at the bay, she was anxious to hear about the dark blue water and what we had discovered. The first thing that Tridax told her was about the pot, and how weird it looked. He really didn't understand what the air pocket was but he did try to describe it to his grandma. Then Trido asked the scouts to explain to Esaw about what they had seen and about the air pocket they had discovered. Esaw said, after dinner!

Tridax was anxious to hear the stories all over again and waited for the Scouts to tell their story. In no time at all the rest of the clan was there ready to listen to the story to! I had to show everybody the gold pot that they had discovered; they passed it around so each of them could check it out. I was anxious to get it cleaned up so I could see what it really looked like. This is it, the bottom was flat and it looked like it had a rose in the middle. The writing and the picture was the same on both sides of the pot.

We enjoyed the rest of the evening with the Roslander Clan, and talked about what we were going to do about the dark water. We wanted to see how big the air pocket really was and why there weren't any dead creatures at the bottom of the pocket. It didn't make any sense that there wasn't any, not that I wanted to see dead creatures. If they swam into the air pocket they would have fallen to the bottom of the pocket. When the scouts went into the dark water, they had ropes that were tied around their waists so they wouldn't fall into the pocket.

We had a plan but it was going to take a lot of preparation before we did it. For the next couple of days, we needed to prepare for the next journey over there. We had to tie more ropes together, we wanted at least three lines, and each had to be 100 feet long, just in case we needed it. Good thing we have been collecting the rope all this time! We knew the air pocket was 15 feet from the top of the dark water to the bottom of the air pocket, and at least 30 to 40 feet deep from what we understood from the Scouts. We also wanted to go into the cave to see what it looked like, so it was going to take a lot of rope. We also found three logs that we tied together; it would be our raft of sorts. The idea was to tie the rope around the logs and then dive off from there, this way we wouldn't have to hold the ropes. Our rubber raft would be tied to that wooden raft.

Everyone was getting excited about going to the dark water it looked like it was going to be a Clan event. Some of the Merbeings were going to swim down along the outside of the air pocket to see how deep and wide it was while we went inside of the air pocket to check it out.

31

EVERYTHING WAS READY, we had our plan, and we had our rope and we were all excited to go check out the dark water. The Merbeings had been checking the dark water out just a little bit, they would swim around the dark water, and stick their arm in to it, but that was it. Because they were told to keep their distances until Trido said it was safe to be around.

It was time for us to go, we pushed the log raft into the bay and the Roslander teenagers started pulling it out of the bay and headed towards the dark water. We put our gear into the rubber raft and started paddling out of the bay and then the scouts grabbed hold of the ropes and started pulling us to the dark water. Again, it is nice to have the Merbeings around to help with the water activities!

It didn't take long to get to the other end of the island and the weather was beautiful, there wasn't a cloud in the sky. We felt that it would be safe enough to go closer to the cliff edge than before. We had the teenagers put the log raft into the middle of the dark water, and then we paddled up to it and tied off the raft. We decided it wasn't a good idea for both of us to go down at the same time. So Frank, Trido and Tride, would go first then if everything was safe I would go down next. As the guys got ready to dive, they needed to tie ropes around their waists, to ensure we could pull them out, if we needed to. The Roslanders clan members that came with us took positions around the edge of the dark water, to watch the show. I felt like we were in an arena waiting to be fed to the lions, or in this case sea monsters! But the scouts guarantee us there were no monsters in the dark water hole.

The guys were gone for quite a while it seemed, Roslanders all had disappeared into the water to watch the show. Esaw and I were left hanging out by the raft waiting to see what was to happen. After awhile we did dive into the dark water with the rest of the clan, to see what we could see, but as they went into the air pocket we couldn't see them anymore from where we were swimming. I didn't think there was any point for me to stay in the water so I climbed out on to the raft, Esaw joined me and we enjoyed the sun until they came back up.

I started seeing Merbeings heads popping up along the edge of the dark water; I figured any moment the guys would pop their heads up too. Then all of a sudden there they were. They all had big smiles on their faces. All Frank could say was it was so cool and I should go next!

As Frank climb onto the raft, and took his gear off, I waited for him to tell me what it was like. Trido and Tride were also smiling and Esaw finally said "Well what happened?" Trido told her "I have never seen anything like it before. It is a big air pocket that is attached to the cliffs; the reason why there are no dead creatures at the bottom of the air pocket is because they would just fall back into the water. It's not a solid wall or a floor, the air just keeps the water from entering that area." Frank joined in and said the bottom is no different than the top. As we came to the top of the air pocket again, we just let go and fell all the way to the bottom and hit the water underneath. It was a lot like skydiving, Frank turned to Trido and Esaw and asked them if they knew what skydiving was, they said no so Frank explained to them that people jump out of planes with parachutes on their backs. He also explained the parachutes would open up into a big tent which would slow them down as they floated to the ground.

After Frank explained to Trido, he agreed that is exactly how it felt. The guys explained to us that they would climb up the rope into the air pocket until they almost got to the top and then they would let loose of the rope and land in the bottom and then go through to the water. It was a great idea to have the ropes on us; otherwise we would've just fallen through to the other side of the air pocket. Granted we could have swam, around to the side of the air pocket and went to the top. It was much more fun to climb up the rope and then drop in.

It was time for Esaw and me to go into the air pocket. Frank helped put my scuba gear on and then the guys tied the ropes around our waists. We were now ready to dive into the dark water. As we descended into the water you could tell that the area where the air pocket seems empty, which makes sense, that's what guys, told us it would look like.

As we got closer we looked at each other and we could tell we were both thinking the same thing, what the hell are we doing! As we got closer to the edge of the air pocket we turned and put our legs first, it was a weird feeling it was the opposite of what you normally feel when you stick your legs in the water and your upper body is out of the water. As we slowly went into the air pocket we held onto our ropes, once we were inside the air pocket, I removed my mask and asked Esaw are you ready, and she replied "let's do it!" I put my mask back on and then we let loose of the ropes and did a freefall through the air pocket. The next thing we knew we were hitting water again. I have to agree with Frank it defiantly felt like skydiving with a mix of cliff diving. After we entered the water at the bottom of the air pocket we were surprised to see the guys were there. I guess, they must have swum around the air pocket, and waited for us to pop out of the pocket.

Esaw and I, started climbing up the rope into the air pocket again as we got up inside of the air pocket we looked down and there were the guys with their heads sticking into the air pocket at the bottom of the air pocket. It was the funniest thing you could ever see. Then all of a sudden we saw other Merbeings coming through the air pocket and landing at the bottom of it. I guess this would be their cliff diving. They couldn't stop inside the air pocket but they could fly through the air and hit the bottom of the pocket. It was weirdest looking thing to see flying Merbeings everywhere.

As we were on our ropes, I started swinging back and forth and Esaw joined in and we swung back and forth inside the air pocket. The ropes were long enough for us to swing from one side of the air pocket to the other. We would hit the wall, and go through it and hit the water and then come back into the air pocket. The difference in temperature wasn't that different. As I hit the water wall, I was wondering how cold it would be, but it wasn't, the temperature inside the pocket was the same as the water outside. I'll have to agree with Frank, it was a very cool place.

What a great place, it was almost like going to a Theme Park. We spent pretty much the rest of the day playing inside the air pocket, but when it started getting a little dark we decided it was time to head back to the bay. We decided to leave the log raft where it was, so we could come back later and investigate the cave and maybe play a little more, if we wanted to. The teenagers had already figured out they could use the log raft to swing from one side of the air pocket to the other, and they would let go of the rope as it a swung into the middle of the pocket. They would go out the bottom and swim around the edge to the raft and do it again. The kids stayed for awhile, but Trido and Esaw went back with us to the bay. Tridax wanted to stay a little longer so Tride had to stay with him. It didn't take much to talk him into it.

The Scout was nice enough to pull us back to the other side of the island, I really wasn't looking forward to paddling back to the bay, and I don't think Frank was either.

Once we got back to the bay, we talked to Trido and Esaw about going back in a couple of days, and checking out the cave inside the air pocket. They agreed now that we know how to use the air pocket to get into the cave, we had a plan. The plan was to move the raft closer to the cave entrance, and then Frank and I would swing from the raft into the cave.

We had a nice dinner with Trido and Esaw, and said our good nights, and headed up to the house. We saw the rest of the clan coming into the bay. It looked like they had a good time. Tride and Tridax waved at us and we waved back. The bed really felt nice, I just wanted to add these notes, tomorrow another fun day to come.

CHAPTER

 **32** 

T TOOK A little bit to get out of bed this morning. I my arms were sore from climbing up and down the rope and swing in the air pocket yesterday. Frank wasn't in too bad a shape, but he swims a lot more than I do. After breakfast we headed down to the bay to see what everybody was up too. There was nobody to be seen; we figured they were still at their city under the water. We decide to go for a walk down the beach, and then for a swim to stretch out and loosen up our muscles. The water here in the afternoon is almost like going into a bathtub, we played in the water for a while, and dived for some sea plants for lunch and maybe even some clams, and of course fish!

One thing Koro had told us is that if we eat too much fish it isn't good for our bodies. But with the sea plants and land plants, it helps keeps our body balanced. We also have a lot of high-protein food in our diets with the chicken and the eggs that we get from the chickens.

One of the dishes I make is eggs with the sea plant and dried land plants, and then I put it on top of the fish and put it in the smoker for about two hours and then it's ready to eat. It has such an unusual flavor to it. I can't remember ever having it back in Texas.

After our swim we went and laid on the beach and just enjoyed the sun until we heard somebody yelling our name, as we sat up we could see, Tride and Tridax wave at us to come over. As we got closer, we noticed there was someone else with them. It was Trigut and the new baby Trien. We were so excited to see them and walked into the water and Trigut automatically handed me Trien, without missing a step, I got to hold her!   What a beautiful little girl, she had blonde hair and the bluest eyes you could imagine. She was a little over a year and a half old, but she was the size of a four-year-old. It's a good thing that the water helped support her weight, although she wasn't that heavy, but with my arms hurting, it did take a little work. Tridax was right there talking a mile a minute about his new sister and how excited he was that they came home early so they could be together. I had asked Trigut why she had come back so early and she told us that she couldn't stand being away from everyone and the baby was doing really well for her age. So she didn't feel that would be any danger in bringing her here early. I was glad that she had decided to do it. We really wanted to see and meet Trien; we both felt like we were the grandparents and it's always exciting to see the new grandkids.

I asked Esaw if her arms were hurting her and she said "yes, she wasn't use to using her arms like that. I guess it is different muscles we use for swimming. She asked if we had a good time, and I told her yes, we did. Let's do it soon! But Frank and I still want to check out the cave that is inside the air pocket. By the looks of it, it must be close to where we found the building we found inside the mountain earlier this month. She asked if we saw anything that looked like a doorway or an entrance way to the outside. I told her no. We'll just have to check it out tomorrow.

I turned to Trigut and started asking her questions about how she was feeling. I couldn't stand it anymore so I asked her how do Mermaids deliver their baby, she just smiled and looked at her mother-in-law, Esaw. We were wondering how long it would take before you asked us. We deliver just like the other mammal in the seas. We just don't do it in open water, we have a place in the city where we can lay and be comfortable until it is time. We can have trouble with the delivery if we have more than two at a time.

Esaw just smiled and said "How do human female deliver their baby?" I just laughed and told her, it's been awhile, and then I explained how we deliver our babies. I told her we normally go to a hospital and a doctor delivers the baby. Of course, I explain what a hospital was and what a doctor was. Esaw said "The delivery of our babies is part of the healer's honor." I never really thought about it to be an honor for a doctor to deliver a baby, but it would be!

Trien wanted to go play with Tridax, so she swam over to him and her dad Tride. Tridax was swimming around her and making little waves for her to play with, kind of like how human kids jump waves, but with their tails and of course in water. Tride came up from under Trien and raised her up into the air, and she made the funniest sound, and then she started laughing. She asked her dad to do it again, and then it was Tridax turn. Tride picked Tridax up and threw him up into the air and then Tridax turned and dived into the water. It was great watching them play and enjoying the day.

We all had our meals together; I know I haven't put this in my journal before, so I wanted to explain how we have a meal together. Frank and I made a table out of bamboo, and it floats in the bay. When we want to have a meal together we anchored the table down so it won't move. Frank and I have set up a couple of rock chairs, and the Roslanders would sit around the bamboo table with us, it is quite a family gathering. When we finish our meal, it is very easy to clear the table off, we just scrape the food into the water and the fish immediately eat it, better than a garbage disposal that we had back home. The plate is a big leaf from a sea plant and we use our finger to eat with. Everything is recycling back into the ocean. At the house it is a little different, we do use plates and silverware, and I put the dishes in a box with big holes, and I put it into the little waterfall that we had built into the creek that we have by our place. I just leave them there until we use them again. Of course, all of the left over goes to the chickens and pigs, and the parrots we have hanging around.

Frank and I said our good nights and went for our walk down the beach; we did this almost every night. After our walk we headed up to the house to play some cards and enjoy the evening. Tomorrow we head back to the dark water and see what is in the cave.

CHAPTER

33

THE NEXT MORNING we got up and started preparing to go back to the dark waters to check out the cave. When we noticed there was a commotion at the bay. We walked down to see what was going on.

Esaw swam up to us and told us that Istin was missing. She is one of the ancient ones that have the power to see the future, but yet she gets a little confused sometimes, after she has done a reading. This is the first time that she has wandered off by herself. We asked Esaw what we could do to help. Esaw asked us to walk along the beach just in case she decided to lie out sunbathing. We headed down to the beach, keeping an eye on the shore line and the beach area. We also checked the different piles of seaweed that had washed ashore the night before. We could see the Roslanders out in the water, swimming, and calling to her. They really were worried about her. I couldn't figure out what could've happened to her.

Then we heard the call of one of the Roslanders farther down the beach, we took off running to see what was going on. On the shore line, there was Istin, laying there; it looks like she had hit her head on something. Koro showed up in no time at all and looked her over. Koro wanted to get her back into the water as fast as she could. I asked if she was okay and Koro said she was a little confused, but she'll be okay.

Frank and I had visited with her a few times in the past. She is a very interesting mermaid, she had many stories to tell us, but her biggest thing was to always be prepared for anything that could happen. She was always telling us to save our food and keep a stash hidden in case we needed it. I really was never sure of what she meant. As far as being on the island, if something happens to the island, I'm pretty sure that we would be done for!

We headed back to the house; it was getting too late to go to the cave today, we planned ongoing tomorrow. For the rest of the day, we just cleaned up the beach and hung out at the bay with the Roslanders.

We were playing in the water with the Roslanders, when we saw Istin coming towards us, which was unusual for her. She normally stayed in the underwater city, and would only come up in the mornings to enjoy the sun. We were hoping that she wasn't having another breakdown or wandering off again. But she swam straight up to Frank and me and told us "You will be leaving this island very soon, and you will safely go home!" Frank asked her "When is this supposed to happen?" All she would tell us is "Only time will tell!" Then she just swam off, back to their underwater city. Frank and I were very confused about what she had said, but excited that maybe someday we will leave this island! She has been known to be very accurate in her fortune-telling; we had no reason to doubt that she was telling us the truth.

Esaw and Trigut swam over to us, and asked us what did Istin say to us? Frank told them what she had told us and all they could say was they would miss us. They acted like it was a fact, and not a prediction of the future. I guess all we can do is wait and see!

Trigut started asking me questions about the museum that we had found earlier this year at the ancient city, the one behind our house at the bay. I had forgotten that she wasn't there when we first discovered the underground museum. I knew how excited she would be to hear about it. So I went and got my Journals from the house. Trigut had so many questions, if she had legs she would have gone to the museum. We talked for hours, I showed her the pictures we had drawn of some of the things we saw. It was getting late so we said our good night and she headed back home and I headed up to the house.

As I was walking up to the house I had an idea, and I knew just the man to ask about it. When I got to the house Frank was already asleep, I guess it was later than I thought. I didn't what to wake him, so I sat outside and worked on my plan.

My plan was to come up with a way for Trigut could go into the museum and see everything. It wouldn't be hard to get her there, Frank could carry her, if need be. But we do have the cart that we had made earlier. We just need to figure out how she could get down the hole and move around inside of the museum. This is where I need Franks help, I guess that's it for tonight.

34

I HAD TALKED TO Frank about what I wanted to do, first thing that morning and he thought it was a great idea. He also pointed out that more than likely Tridax would want to go too. I agreed with him, Tridax always wanted to go on adventure with us. After a little bit, Frank had come up with a few ideas, he didn't think it was a good idea for him to carry Trigut, he didn't know if it would cause problems for her and they were kind of slippery, and he would hate to drop her in the woods. He had already figure out pretty much everything by noon. That's my man, the inventor! By the sounds of it, it will take a couple of days to get everything ready. We agreed we wouldn't tell Trigut anything until we were ready to put the plan into action. I was about the same size as Trigut, so I will be the test person (I'm not putting down dummy).

First we cleared a path to the entryway of the museum; we already had a cart that Frank had made awhile ago. All he had to do is work on making it more comfortable to ride in, and easier to manage.

We spent the day up in the woods, getting the rope we needed together. We did most of the work by the ancient city, so we wouldn't have to carry everything there later.

As the evening fell we went down to the bay for a swim and enjoy the evening with the Roslanders. We had a pretty good workout today so we really didn't feel like doing much. Tride swam over to Frank and asked what we had been up to all day, because they hadn't seen us. Frank just told him we were looking around the ancient city and making sure that the museum was not leaking where we had done the patch work earlier this year, and everything looked pretty good. About that time Trigut had swam over to visit with us too and she asked if the museum was okay and I had told her yes. Then she said "I wish I could see it for myself, it sounds so wonderful!" All I could do is look at Frank and smile, and told her I wish you could to!

After a while Frank and I decided to go on our normal evening walk together and make plans for the next day. Tride had also asked when we planned on going back to the dark waters, and Frank had told him in a couple days. He was in the middle of fixing some things up around the house.

Tride had told Frank that the teenagers have been going back to the dark waters and playing off the raft that we had left there. They also had swam up to the cave area to see if they could find anything else, but there really wasn't much else in there as far as they could see. They did say when the tide came in, they were able to swim inside of the cavern, and it looked like there might have been an opening at the back of the cavern at one time. There is a crack in the wall that looked like it may have been an entry way at sometime. This of course got Frank interested in going back to the dark water sooner than later. But we both agreed that it was more important to show Trigut the museum.

When we got back to the house; we decided to work on the rope swing that we were going to use to lower Trigut and Tridax down into the museum. We also made wheelchairs, so they could move about in the museum.

The next morning we gave the swing rope a try. The idea was that Frank would lower me into the hole and I would have to keep my legs together, as if I had a tail instead of legs, to make sure that it was exactly how it would happen with Trigut.

When we lower Trigut and Tridax down into the museum, I would be at the bottom of the hole to help Trigut and Tridax get into their wheelchairs that we had made for them. We had made two wheelchairs, one for each of them. Well they were kind of a wheelchair. The only difference was there were no wheels, and we would us bamboo rails and put whale oil on the rails, this would help move the wheelchair along in the museum. What we would do is use a bamboo pole, which is hooked to the chair, so we can pull them around, we could also push them along too. This way they could see all of the artifacts on display that are in the museum.

After a couple of days we had tested everything to make sure Trigut and Tridax would be safe. The cart that Frank had fixed up for them, so we could get them to the entry way and be comfortable. In testing everything Frank did a great job of pulling me around, I felt like a Queen. Then he carried me to the hole and put me into the rope swing and lowered me to the wheelchair, then pulled me with the bamboo pole. Everything worked great! I felt great but I think Frank was getting a little tired of doing all the work. When I asked him how he was doing he said "I just keep thinking how wonderful it will be for Trigut and Tridax to see the museum. It makes me feel great!"

After working most of the day getting things ready, we went down to the bay to relax for awhile. We tried to act like nothing was going on but the Roslanders knew something was up, they couldn't tell what it could be. We told them we had a surprise for Trigut and Tridax, but we wanted to wait until tomorrow to show them. After our swim we decided to skip our walk, Frank was pretty tired. We headed up to the house for the night. I needed to work on the ropes a little more, I had found a few places that needed repairs, but we were ready for tomorrow. Frank fell right to sleep, who can blame him!

CHAPTER

35

TODAY WAS THE big day; we pushed the cart down to the bay, where the Roslanders were waiting for us. Tridax was the first to ask why we had the cart. Frank told him it was their surprise. He just looked at us and then his parents. Then Frank turned to me and said "Are you going to tell them?" He always likes making a big production out of things.

I walked over to Trigut and told her the cart is for you. We want to take you to the museum, and if Tridax wants to go we can take him too.

She just looked at us in shock and didn't say anything for a moment. Then Tridax said "Can we Mom?" She looked at him and then at us again, she finally said "Really? How? Now?" Frank responded, "We have it all planned out."

We'll push the cart into the water and you and Tridax can get in and then we'll push you up to the museum entrance and then lower you into the hole with a swing we have made out of rope. We have made chairs that move, so we can move you around inside the museum.

Well what do you say? I asked Trigut. Tridax swam over to his Mom and asked "Can we Mom?" I think she was still in shock, but then she said. "Yes, thank you for doing this." Tride came over to her and gave her a hug, and Tridax went out and did a flip in the water.

Frank said "Well let's get you into the cart." He pushed the cart to the water's edge and then had her put a blanket around her tail, then he picked her up and had her sit at the end of the cart, then he loaded Tridax in next to her.

Once we had them settled into the cart, we started pushing it up towards our house. It was a lot of work pushing the cart threw the sand in the beginning, but we had the foresight to build a stone path a while ago, it went up to our house. Frank also had cut some bamboo in half and put the wheel inside of it, the wheel would just roll inside the bamboo, until we got to the stone path. We had found the stones when we were building our house, we think at one time it was a courtyard of some kind. It almost went to the water edge; we have never found the edge of it. The ancient city was only about 25 feet from our house, but the museum was another 50 feet. So we did have a little ways to go to get to the entry way.

Tridax was having a great time; he has never been this far on the beach and had never been close to living trees. Trigut looked a little more nervous, but she was excited about seeing the museum and willing to do whatever it took to go see it. As we were pushing the cart, we got stuck one time, but we tied a rope to the cart and then put it around a tree by the house. We both pulled until the cart was free from the hole that it had gotten stuck in. Then we continued on our journey.

We finally reached the opening of the museum; Frank carried Trigut to the entry way of the museum first. I went down below and waited for her to come down through the hole. Frank waited for me to let him know that it was okay to lower her, and Tridax. It was really weird seeing a mermaid on a swing in midair. Trigut was great; she just smiled and wanted to see what was going to happen next. Once she was lowered into the wheelchair, I took her out of the swing and Frank pulled the swing back up the hole, so he could lower Tridax down next. Tridax didn't stop asking questions the whole way, things like, how does this work or why did we do that and so forth. He was pretty excited about the new adventure.

Trigut watched as Frank lowered Tridax into the museum, you could tell she was very nervous about the whole thing. I was waiting for him to be lowered down the hole, so I could put him into his chair. I could tell that Trigut wanted to help, but all she could do is watch. I settled Tridax into his wheelchair, and we waited for Frank to come down the stairs. But instead, he came down the hole on the rope. Once Tridax was down, Trigut felt much better and started looking around the museum. I could see her mind going a mile a minute. We settled both of them into their chairs, and grabbed the poles so we could pull them to the rail.

Frank asked Trigut and Tridax "Are you ready to see the museum?" They both yelled "YES!" This is the first time I have ever seen, Trigut so excited, she was like a little kid in a candy store. I told her to let us know when to start or stop as we moved around the museum. She asked if it would be okay to touch things, and I told her I don't think it would be a problem. I don't think you could hurt anything down here at this point. But I wouldn't touch anything inside of the cases, because we wouldn't want to let the air in. She agreed!

Once we were in the main area we could push the wheelchairs, instead of pull them. We had to pull the chairs out of the loading area because there was nothing else we could do; there wasn't enough room to pull rails in the small area. Once we were in the main museum we could use the rails. This way we could push the wheelchairs, instead of pulling them, it worked great, there was no problems. Trigut was pointing at one thing and then another. Tridax was doing the same!

The best part, we found out is that she knew a lot of what she was looking at. As I had mentioned in my earlier journal, Trigut loves history! Her family has passed down history of the planet, from her ancestors from generation to generation.

When we connected telepathically awhile back, she had showed me all the wonderful things that they had had in the castle under the sea. She could even read some of the writing that was underneath some of the pictures and plates in the museum. (Note to self, I need to show the writing from the theater room that we had discovered earlier this year.)

As we moved along, Tridax had all kinds of questions, he was really interested in everything that he saw, and he continued to ask his mom about different things. I guess he takes after his mom when it comes to history.

Trigut was telling us about the different items, after she read the writing underneath the different artifacts. It was great to have Trigut there. We thought we were the ones showing Trigut something new and different, but it ended up being her telling us about the wonderful things in the museum.

Frank asked Trigut "How do you know so much about the things that happened on land?" Trigut told us "There are many human cities under the water. There is one city that my ancestors used to visit when it was still on land, when they still had water ways, going into their cities. They had learned the humans' language and the way they lived.

Then the city started to sink, it was the way it started to sink that wasn't normal. It sunk very quickly but didn't damage the city at all; it was as if it was being protected, from the water force, it was being pulled under the water. It sits in the bottom of the ocean, pretty much the way it was above the water. But now small and large ocean creatures live in it.

Trigut continued with telling us that her family would go there and explored the different building; they wanted to learn more about the ways of the humans that used to live there." As we approached the room where the mummies were, Trigut and Tridax got quiet. We got as close as we could so they could get a good look at each of them. Then they raised themselves on their tails, so they could see more details.

Tridax again was the first to ask who they were, and I asked Trigut, can you read what is on the markers? Out of the five mummies, she could read four of them. The fifth one was not a language she knew. This made sense to us because they didn't look like any of the other mummies, which were displayed. It did look humanoid but not like a normal human being or even a Merbeing. We think it was one of the star people or the ones they called green ones.

I want to explain about the mummies, they all were inside Plexiglas. Thing is, it wasn't real Plexiglas it was seamless and look like it was of one unit. The bodies inside of these display boxes, looked like they had been there for a very long time. Each of the mummies was in different states of deterioration.

It was obvious which one was a Merbeing, because of the tail. The interesting thing about it was if you looked at the bone structure there were two bones going down, they look just like our leg bones. It's as if they were legs tied together and then where our feet were suppose to be, the bones at the end of the tail was fanned out. If you smashed your foot sideways and spread it out, that is what it looked like inside their tail. So maybe we are a lot closer to the Merbeing race than we know.

The second mummy's bones were thicker than the other human body. Trigut said, "That this is the human that lived in the city, she had told us about her earlier."

I asked her if she would tell us about the other four, she said "She would love to!" This is what Trigut told us about mummies:

"The mummy that was the Merbeing was a great leader, he and Torhe (the first human mummy) work together to keep peace between the different species. The other three mummies that were on display were also great leaders." The third one was a woman who was seven foot tall; we measured her to be sure. Frank and I called her the Amazon women; she was not only tall, but very fit. The fourth mummy was about four foot tall, but her head was bigger, than the rest, she was the smallest of the five of them. The fifth one was the star being, well, we are calling it a star being. This mummy looked like a human, but had a large head, and big eyes like the merbeings but larger, its body was smaller than all the rest of the mummies. The big different between it and the other mummies was it didn't have any possessions with it. All that was there was its body, and we couldn't tell what sex it was.

Trigut had read all of the plaques on the display coffins; she told us what was written on them. From what I understand, we were right that these were all great leaders. Trigut said, "Each of them had a job to do, and all five had to agree on each changes or problems that needed to be resolved for the community and the planet. They were not rulers, but counselors for the beings of the world. But when the planet started to change, the beings of the world started going their separate ways and causing more chaos than ever before. They stopped communicating with each other and in time lost touch with each other, and the connection with the planet. But they had hoped that someday this museum would be found. That being's would know that it is possible; all could live together in peace.

36

WE SPENT ALL day in the museum looking at all the displays and asking Trigut questions, she read the different plaques and telling us about what they said about the artifacts that we were looking at. It is much more interesting when you know what you are looking at! But it was time to leave, I helped Trigut get into the rope swing, and I went and joined Frank to pull her up. It was much easier to lower her, than it was to raise her up. Of course, I didn't help lower her, so that would be easier for me anyway. As she came out of the hole I grabbed the rope and pulled her into the cart and then removed the rope swing from her.

I headed down to get Tridax, when I heard Frank yell out in pain. I turned to see him on the ground. I called down to Tridax, I'll be right there, something is wrong with Frank. He called back, "Okay, I'm fine!" I ran back over to Frank and he was just lying there in pain. Trigut asked "Is he okay?" He was just laying there, moaning and grabbing his back. I cleared out the brush around him so he could lay flat but other than that it wasn't much I could do for him at this point. I sat down next to him and asked what I could do and what was hurting him? In a painful voice, he said

"I think I pulled a muscle in my back!" The first thing I thought of was the berry plant I used before on him, the Hanri plant. The only problem was it was out of season. I asked Trigut if they had anything Frank could take and she told me to go ask Koro, she was sure she would have something to help. I was getting ready to run down to the bay, when I remember Tridax was still in the museum. Frank told me "Go get Tridax and then we can pull him up, by this time Frank was sitting up against a tree. He told me he could hold the rope, after I pulled him up, as if he could read my mind, he said "yes, I am sure!" I headed down to the museum, and I put Tridax into the swing rope and then I ran back up to Frank and Trigut to pull Tridax up.

When I got over to Frank and Trigut, Frank was standing up next to the cart and Trigut had her hands on his back. She was doing energy healing on him. It seemed to be helping him! He looked better. Well a little better anyway. He wanted to help pull Tridax up and I told him I could do it. Using the pulley that Frank had set up earlier, when we lowered them into the museum. I just needed his help to hold the rope, while I unloaded Tridax. It didn't take long to get Tridax up and loaded into the cart.

The next problem is getting them back to the water. But I had a plan, if we could get them to the house I could run ropes down to the water. Then Tride and his friends could pull the cart to the water.

After explaining my plan, Frank said he could help move them to the bay. It wouldn't be that hard, it was flat and the cart was easy to push. As we pushed the cart, Trigut started to apologize, Frank told her to stop, it was our idea, and we really enjoyed hearing all of the information she had told us!"

I tried to do most of the pushing, but Frank was right there to help as much as he could. We finally made it to the beach! I went down to the water and Tride and Trido were there. I could tell they were a little anxious about where Trigut and Tridax were. I told them what had happened and my plan to get Trigut and Tridax back to the water. Trido called to a few of the Merbeings for help. I went and got the rope we needed, Frank worked on connecting the rope to the cart and then I took the other end to the Roslanders. I handed the rope to Tride and everyone else took a hold of the rope. It looked like we were going to have a tug a war. They were lined up in the bay, ready to pull. I called up to Frank, are you ready and he called back "Go for it! The Roslanders started pulling, I ran up to the cart, just in case, the cart tried to leave the stone path, or turn over. It started to move off the path, but I would just push it back onto the path, and it would go right back on with no problem. This time they could pull the cart all the way into the water. Once the cart was in the water Trigut and Tridax just swam out.

The whole time, Tridax was having a great time, he wasn't even in the water yet, and he was telling his dad all about the museum, how cool it was and mom could read everything. Tride looked at Trigut and smiled and said, "Of course." Finally, Trigut and Tridax were in the water again. Tridax asked if he could go tell his friends all about today's adventure, and Trigut said "Yes". Tridax turned to me and thanked me and said "Tell Frank thank you too!" That's when I noticed Frank wasn't there; I turned and saw him just lying on the beach. I called to him, are you okay? He put his arm up in the air, and gave me a thumbs-up.

About that time, is when Koro showed up, she had already been informed about what had happened, and had brought some herbs and potions, that she thought would help Frank feel better. I called up to Frank to let him know I hadn't forgotten him. Koro handed me a couple of things to give Frank. One of the items was a green mussel, which was very oily. She instructed me to put the oil on his muscle area that was hurting, and takes two of the mussel and cut them into small pieces and put it into a tea for Frank to drink. The herb plants were to go on different points of his body. It was a sticky patch, so it was going to be easy for it to stick to him. Koro said "After placing the herbs on his back, cover them with cloth to protect them from being pulled off." I thanked her and headed up to see how Frank was doing.

I walked over to where Frank was laying; he had wiggled himself down into the sand. It was the funniest thing I have seen in awhile. I asked him what happened. He smiled and said "The sand was so warm, I just kept moving down, it's wonderful, it is so warm, and it likes having a warm sand bed to lie on. As long as I don't move my back it doesn't hurt, so I'm good here!"

Frank you know you are going to have to get out of the hole, you can't lie there all night, and it's going to get cold pretty soon. Beside, Koro has given me some herb and oil for you; it will fix you up in no time. He just said "In a little bit, it still nice and warm in here. I could hear Tride calling to me "What happen to Frank?" He was standing on his tail so he could see us, up on the beach. I told Frank I'll be right back, he said "Take your time!" and raised his arm and gave me the thumbs up again. I just laughed and walked back to the bay, to let them know what was going on.

Tride and Trigut looked puzzled as I walked up to them. Trigut asked where Frank was, I told them he's Ok, his enjoying the heat from the sand. He wiggled himself down in the sand, about three inches; it's going to be fun, trying to pull him out of the hole. But for now he's not in pain and is very happy there.

They both laughed and Trigut told me how much they both enjoyed themselves today. Trigut was just so sorry that Frank hurt himself. I told her he'll be fine. Koro spoke up and told me, that I needed to get Frank out of the sand hole; the sand will start pulling the heat out of his body, as the evening approaches.

I thanked her and headed back up to Frank. Yea he was still there, sound asleep! I woke him and told Frank what Koro had told me about how the sand will suck the heat from his body, and he replied "Yeah, I am getting kind of cold!"

I helped him sit up, and the pain in his back started in again. I told him, we could use the cart like a walker to get him up to the house and get him settled in for the night. I had pulled the cart close to him earlier, so he could use it to help with standing up and I grabbed the other side of him, to pull him up. Frank was ready to stand up, he got on his hands and knees first and then he used the cart to support himself. Together, we were able to get him standing again. I could tell that he was in great pain, but there wasn't much else we could do till I get him to the house.

It took us a little while but we finally got him up to the house and I prepared the herbs that Koro had given me earlier. He sat there for a little bit, and drank his tea and then I made him some dinner, because we hadn't eaten much today. Then I had him lay on the bed so I could put the sticky wraps on his body, then put a T-shirt back on him.

Frank barely got through dinner, when he started falling asleep, I guess the herb and oils were working. I cleaned up and covered him up and he was out. It had been a long day, so I wasn't far from hitting the sack either. We both must've been exhausted; the next thing I hear is the birds singing and I saw Frank sitting at the table. He had already made tea and eggs for breakfast.

I was surprised to see him up, I asked if he was okay, he said "I have a little pain, but the herbs and oil really worked great! But I think I need to take it easy for a couple of days." I agreed with him, so I carried the tea to the chairs in front of the house, so we could enjoy the morning air. I turned to him and said you couldn't have a better view! We could see the Bay and down the beach for miles from where we sat. The Roslanders were out doing their daily life chores. We saw Tridax waving at us, so we waved back. After a while Frank wanted to walk down to the bay and stretch out his back a little.

Nothing like soaking in the big tub of warm water, the bay was always nice and warm. He did pretty well, he was slow but we did make it to the bay. The Roslanders were waiting for us, and anxious to see how Frank was doing. Trido and Esaw were the first to greet us, and asked how he was doing. He told them he was fine, just a little sore. Esaw told him she had sent for Koro, so she could check him out and make sure there wasn't anything else she could do for him. As we waited for her to show up, we moved into the deeper water, Frank wanted to float and relax his back while we waited.

37

DURING ALL OF the excitement I had forgotten to close up the entry way to the museum. It looked like there was a storm coming in, I wanted to make sure that it was sealed up, before the storm hit. Frank wanted to help, but I told him no, it wouldn't be that hard to do and I didn't want him to mess up his back again. He walked me up to the house, and said he would sit there and listen if I needed help, he would hear me. I agreed with him. That was a good plan. But I also warned him not to move from the chair while I was gone! He just smiled and nodded his head. He wouldn't move.

I headed off to the museum entryway, and started working on moving the cover back over the hole, when I heard something down inside the hole; something was inside of the museum. I had to go find out what it was, I couldn't just leave it inside, whatever it was. I went down the staircase, I could hear a funny sound, and I wasn't quite sure what it was. But I was pretty sure it wasn't something big and strange hiding in the museum that I couldn't deal with. Well at least I was hoping it was nothing to worry about.

As I moved closer to the sound, I recognized what it was. It was three chickens that had fallen into the hole, and were running around the museum like they owned the place. All I could think of was great! I need to get these things out of here, before they do any damage. So the chase began, I finally trap one of them, and caught it. I carried it up to the forest and then went down for the other two, as I'm yelling here chick, here, here chick and swearing a little bit. I heard this laughter above me and I looked up and there was Frank with a big grin on his face, he asked me "Are you having fun!" Then he disappeared, I went back to chasing the chickens, when I heard Frank call down to me. "Hey, use this!" It was the net we used to catch the chicken in the forest. I cornered the last two and threw the net on top of them. Then I took one at a time up to the top and let them go. Frank was enjoying the show, as I climbed out of the museum; he asked "Do you want chicken for dinner tonight?" Now he asked after I let them go. Men!!

Frank did help me close up the museum, and then we went back to the house for lunch. Frank was doing much better, and he had been talking to Trido and Tride about going to the dark water again. It's been awhile, but the Roslanders teens have been going there and having fun with the swing and water diving into the dark water. Water diving is what they are calling it, instead of sky diving. They wanted us to come join them and show us the acrobatics they are doing.

Frank told them that we would head over there tomorrow, and plan on staying the night. We wanted to get out to the beach and see if anything new had wash up on the beach in the last few months. It's kind of like going shopping, but it doesn't cost any money. The rest of the day, we went fishing and getting some food smoked for the trip. Frank went out and got us a couple of lobsters for dinner, also some clams.

We hadn't played cards in awhile, so we asked Trido and Esaw if they wanted to play cards with us. We had taught them how to play cards awhile ago, the water was a problem in the beginning but with the floating table, it was much easier to do it. After playing a couple of hands, we headed off to bed. We knew it was going to be a long couple of days; we had everything all packed and ready for the trip tomorrow. Frank's back was must better, but I wanted to put more oil on him, to make sure he would be fine for the trip tomorrow.

We were going to have to get up pretty early the next morning to get around the cliff, that's when the tide will be out. Otherwise, we would have to go around the mountain, which was a lot more travel and work for us. We couldn't take the cart with us if we went through the woods.

We had everything packed, but we wanted to double check before we headed off to bed. We were taking ropes, two hammocks, our pillows, food and water, our air tanks and a few other odds and ends! Check and check, I think we're ready for our next adventure!

38

W E WENT TO sleep talking about the dark water and what kind of acrobats the Roslanders had been up to. Trido also offered to take the raft in the morning, which was full of our scuba gear to the site, this way we wouldn't have to carry it all in our cart.

When we woke up the next morning, the sun was just rising, we had time to eat and wake up a little bit before we headed down the beach. We went and checked on the raft, and check-in with Tride.

Tride and Tridax were there waiting for us down at the bay. Tride asked, if there was anything else we wanted to add to the raft, we told him no. Tride looked at Tridax and told him "Are you ready?" Tridax gave him thumbs up; I laughed and looked at Frank, and said I wonder where he got that from! Frank just smiled, and then Tride gave us thumbs up too! Off they went.

We started pushing the cart around the cliff, when we saw something large and red, moving on the beach. It almost looked like a red carpet, but it was moving. We had no clue what it could be, but that never stopped us from investigating things before.

Once we were around the cliff, we pushed the cart closer to the woods, we didn't want the tide coming in and taking the cart away. Then we walked closer to the mass, as we got closer, we could tell that it was red crabs. As we approach the crabs, they turned towards us and their claws went up in the air. I guess they were looking for a fight! The mass covered the whole beach in front of us, from the woods to the shore, and was about fifty feet across. I asked Frank, how are we going to get around them? Then I came up with an idea. I explained to Frank about my idea and he agreed it was a good idea, that's one for me. Nice to know I can come up with ideas once in a while!

What we did is, we put a net around the cart, and it went all the way down to the ground. Then we put sticks in the bottom of the net, this made it into a plow of sorts. We would walk behind the cart and let the cart do all the work. It was working great so far, it is like a little snowplow pushing the crabs out of the way.

It's amazing how the crabs move together, as the cart pushed the crabs, they would move in unison out of the way. We walked behind the cart, as we move forward; they would close up behind us. I felt like I was being followed! There had to be thousands of them, when we looked at the waves coming on to the shore, we could see the waves were red. The crabs were coming in on the surf.

We were surrounded by them! The net plow was working great, but it did make me a little nervous being in the middle of all these crabs, if we fall, we could be done for. There were all sizes, and they moved as if they were one unit. We heard about this type of thing before, the crabs migrate on to the land, and lay their eggs and then go back into the ocean. But being in the middle of it is a whole different feeling.

We went nice and slow and we finally made it in to the other side of the mass. We took the plow off the cart and looked back before we headed down the beach. We continued to look back, to make sure they were not following us, thank goodness they didn't. It seems like every time we come to this side of the island, we see something new and different going on.

We still had a ways to go, we stopped and looked at the piles on the beach, most of it was junk. When we come home we'll have some cleaning up to do. Frank and I agreed in the beginning, we would keep the island beaches clean. It is the least we could do for the island it has kept us safe all these years.

The crabs had put us behind schedule, so we didn't stop and look at all the piles, but we did find a pail, and it looked like it was in pretty good shape. It even had the handle on it. This is a huge win for us!

We arrived late afternoon, to the dark water. The Roslanders were hanging out on the raft and the beach enjoying the sun. They do love their sun bathing! Tride asked us, "What took you so long." I just smiled and said we had a run in with some crabs. Tride replied "Oh, I guess I should have told you about them, they should be gone by the time you go back. Their normally here for about a week, then they disappear into the ocean. But they are really good to eat; maybe we can have crabs tonight for dinner." Frank said "Sounds like a good idea!"

Tridax wanted us to go into the water with him, but we needed to set up camp before we could do anything else. Frank looked a little disappointed but he knew I was right. It didn't take long to get camp setup; the fire pit was still there from the last time we were here. We put our hammocks up and had lunch before we headed back down to the water. Our raft that had our water gear was on the beach already. We got our gear on, and started swimming out to the dock, that we had left here from before. We notice there were two other docks floating on the dark water.

When we arrived to the dark water, there was only a couple of Roslanders sitting on the dock. We asked them where everyone was; they pointed down towards the middle of the dark water, and stated they were watching the show!

We jumped back into the water and swam over to the edge of the dark water; we started swimming along the edge, until we saw the Roslanders. As we swam down we could see the Roslanders, they were on the outside of the air pocket. All we could see was their bottom half of their body; the upper part was inside the air pocket. It was the weirdest looking thing I've seen in a long time, as we got closer we could see into the air pocket. It looked like there was a circus going on. The Roslanders had added more swings and ropes to do other acrobats.

We stuck our heads into the pocket, like everyone else was doing. We saw Tride and Trigut were out on the swings. As we were watching them, Tridax came over to hang out with us. The first thing he asked us was, "Do you see, my mom and dad out there?" He pointed towards them. We told him yes and their great! As we watched the show, we took off our air tanks; we didn't need them, while our heads were in the air pocket. We did have to keep kicking our legs to stay in one place, which was a lot of work after awhile. We could tell Tride and Trigut had been doing this for a while, and they were really good at it.

They had trampoline acts, and they did all kind of things. They would come through the side of the air pocket at a fast rate of speed, and then grab the swing and do a flip and catch the next swing and then do another flip and then fly out of the air pocket, on the other side. Then there were Merbeings jumping from the top of the air pocket and then swinging to the side of the air pocket back into the water. It was amazing to watch, you could tell everyone was enjoying the show. We were looking forward to trying the bungee thing tomorrow. I don't think we can do any of the other things they were doing.

It was time for us to go back to the surface, after a while our legs were getting a little tired. When we surfaced, it was already getting dark, so we headed to the shore. My legs were killing me, but it was a wonderful thing to see, everyone doing their different acts. I don't think they would coincide they acts, but that's what I'm going to call them. It was great to watch!

Frank walked up to the fire pit and started a fire, and it looked like it was going to be a pretty good one. Then Trido and Esaw showed up, they called to us, "We have dinner!" We walked down to the shoreline, where they were sitting. They held up two nets with crabs. Frank said "I'll go get the bucket," and he ran off to go get it. It didn't take long for the bucket that we found, to come in handy.

Trido and Esaw like the way we cooked our crabs, we boiled them in water. Whereas, they would kill the crabs and lay them on the rocks to let the sun cook them slowly. Our way is much faster and juicier than letting the sun cook them, because it would be dry, more liking beef jerky. We tried it once, and that was enough for us.

Frank came back with the bucket, and Trido and Esaw put the crabs into the bucket. Then Tride, Trigut and Tridax swam up and they had some more crabs, and some sea plants to go with them, kind of like a salad. Frank said "I'm going to need a bigger pot!"

Frank grabbed the crabs from Tride and Trigut, and headed back up to the fire. I excused myself and told them I was going to go help Frank and we'll be right back. We had a bigger pot that we had found out in the forest earlier this year. I helped Frank put it on the fire and then he dumped the crabs into it, and I ran down to get more water. As I got down to the shore, there were more Roslanders and more crabs to be cooked, I guess were having a crab fest!

A couple of them went and got the two floating docks, we had out in the water and pushed them over to the shore, this way we could have someplace to put all of the cooked crabs.

This remind me of the crab fest we used to have with our family, we would go out on our boats and come back with a load of crabs and then the next thing we knew we had family and friend coming out of the wood work. It was kind of like today, but these were all merbeing. It was wonderful!

Anyway, Frank and I had to do all the leg work, Ha! Ha! We would cook a pile of the crabs and take them down to the water edge and they would pass them down to the end of the dock. Man, I wish I had a camera. The docks were pretty much a floating table, and there were merbeing all around the dock/table, they were Merbeings sitting, eating the crabs and salad, you don't see that every day! At least I won't have to clean up the tables.

Finally, Frank and I sat down to eat our crabs, we enjoy talking to the Roslanders, and they loved to tell stories of their adventures and how much fun they have been having with the air pocket. All of the teenagers were in agreement; they couldn't wait until the next Batjak, they wanted to show their friends.

Almost all the crabs were gone, when a couple of teenager volunteered to go get more, so off they went. I told Frank we're going to need more wood if we are going to cook more crabs. I know I could eat another one, I love fresh crab; life can't get much better than this. Frank and I headed up to the forest to get more wood, and had the fire going good, when the teenager arrived back with a lot more crabs. We collected them all up, and started the process all over again. We'll be sleeping well tonight!

After the crab fest, they turned the table over to clean it and then pushed it back to where they had it before and now it's a dock again. They said their good nights and headed back to their city. Frank and I headed up to the hammocks, to enjoy the rest of the evening.

THE NEXT THING I knew it was morning. Frank wasn't up yet, so I went to get some fresh water and clean up a little. When I got back, Frank had the fire going and heating up the left over crabs.

The Roslanders told us they would be back around noon, so we enjoyed the morning. We went for a walk and then went to see if the hole we discover earlier this year was still there. We couldn't find it anywhere, we were sure we knew where it was, this is a weird place, is all I can say! We came back to camp and waited for the Roslanders to show up. Just like clockwork, they started showing up. Trido came over and asked us if we were ready to have some fun. Frank said "Of course, but we want to check out the cave while the tide was in, and then we'll head out to the dark water."

Trido said "We'll go with you, we can swim to the back of the cave, when the tide is in, and there are levels of rocks for us to climb up on. Frank told him that would be great. Trido asked if it would be ok if Tride and Tridax came along, they always wanted to go exploding with us. We laughed and said the more the merrier! He called to them, and next thing you know, the family was all there, including Esaw and Trigut.

Frank and I had to put our water gear on, and then we headed over to the cave. Trido said "Follow me, and I'll show you how we have been getting into it." We dived down about six feet, and then headed to the cave. When we entry the cave we were right on the bottom of the cave. It was no different than other caves, it had sea urchin, including starfish, big ones! We climbed up on the rocks, to get to the flat area of the cave. It looked like a path, and it went all around the cave, it looked man made.

Once we were up on the path, we took our water gear off, and started looking around. The Roslanders climbed up on the flat rocks at the end of the cave, and called to us and were pointing at the cave wall. Trido said "This is where we found the crack that looks like an entrance. We walked over to where they were at and looked at the crack, they were right; it looked like a huge entrance way for something. The highest point had to be 30 feet high, and from one side to the other had to be 50 feet. If I didn't know better it looked like a landing dock for something.

We continue to look around but there wasn't anything else to find. Esaw told us that the green ones may have made the cave and the air pocket. The ancient one had told her parents about how they would have a thing that looked like a dish, they would come from the sky, and in the beginning they would fly into the mountain and disappear into the mountain. As the land started to sink they had to make the air pocket. They would dive into the water and hit the air pocket then go into the cave and into the mountain.

Frank and I really didn't know what to say. We know the green ones or the Star being were real. We saw the remains of one in the museum. I finally said, well that interesting, it really doesn't surprise me. Frank agreed and said, "Let's go play in the air pocket. We put the water gear on and headed over to join the rest of the Roslanders. Trido said, "He would lead the way; it could be very dangerous trying to get out of here." When the waves came in they would hit the rocks, and go every which way.

Once we were out of the cave we surfaced by the dock. We wanted to try the dungaree jumping, well it kind of like that. We climbed up on the dock, and Tride was there to show us how to hold the rope and told us what to do.

The plan was to jump off the dock; we would jump into the water straight legged, we would hold on to the rope, the rope was long enough to go half way thought the air pocket and once we were at the end of the rope, we would swing to the side of the air pocket, and hit the water and then let go of the rope.

Frank and I were going to jump together he was going to swing out one side and I was going to swing out the other. We counted to three and jumped. Going thought the water was no big deal, but as I got closer to the air pocket I started going faster, like it was pulling me into it. Then I hit the air pocket and started to fall as if I was sky diving, then the rope came to an end, and jerked. Then I started swing towards the air pocket wall, and then splash I hit the water, feet first. All I can say is WoW!

I swam up to the surface, and Frank was already there. He had a big smile on his face. All he said, "That was so cool! We swam over to the dock where Trido, Esaw and Trigut were waiting for us. Trido asked, "So what do you think?" We both started talking, it was great. Esaw said "To bad you can't do the side entry, it's a lot of fun too! I told her I wish we could do it to. We just can't swim that fast. After a little while, we did another jump, and it was better than the first time, now we knew what to expect. When we came up this time, we headed to the beach, it was getting late.

Trido and his family joined us, we talked about the air pocket and the cave, and that they will be leaving for Utopia soon, but

Trido said the counsel wanted to talk to us before they left. Frank and I looked at each other and wonder what was going on. We said, that is fine, we should be back to the bay in a couple of days, will that be alright? Trido said, "That will be fine, we need to head home, so we'll see you in a couple of days." Everyone said their good-bye's and we head up to the camp. We were going to have dried food tonight, neither one of us felt like making dinner.

As we lay in our hammocks, we talked about the day and wonder what Trido had planned for us. Maybe they are tired of us, and maybe they want us to move to the other side of the island, or we can't hang out with them anymore. It's going to be a long two days.

The next morning we packed up, and cleaned up the camp area. We refilled the water jugs, and were getting ready to head back home. It was a mini vacation with the Roslanders. It was fun to play in the air pocket and having the big crab fest.

Frank and I had talked about how weird it would be to see a space ship come out of the sky and go under the water, into the air pocket and go into the cave. Good news was we didn't see anything like that.

We decide to go for a swim before we leave, it was a little before noon and it was already getting hot. We headed down to the water edge. The water was warm; it was more like going into a big bathtub. Frank was ahead of me and dove into the water. I was just getting ready to dive in, when all of a sudden I felt this pain. I looked down and I could see a large shape moving away from me, and then I fell over, and hit the water with a splash. All I can remember is screaming for help. I was scared, I had no idea what was going on and then I just started crawling towards the beach.

About that time Frank surfaced, he had no clue what had happened to me, but I wasn't sure either. I called to him; I need your help and was waving at him crazily. He knew instantly that I was in trouble and started swimming towards me. When he stood up in the water, I could tell his face was filled with concern. He knew I was in trouble. As he came up to me, he could tell I was in pain, he just didn't know why. I pointed down to my leg where there were two small holes. I told him I don't know what got me! Frank carried me farther up the beach, to get me away from the water's edge.

Then the pain really started, it felt like electricity going down my leg and then coming back up, each time it was getting worse. It didn't take long before I was yelling out in pain, I couldn't even get up. Frank told me, I know what it was, that hit you. It swam right by me, while I was under water. It was a large stingray, if I had to guess, I think it might have been a manta ray or something like that, it was huge, and you must've of stepped on it or scared it.

The pain continued and seemed to be getting worse. I asked Frank, if he knew what we can do to get rid of the pain? He said, "He had no clue, but he will call the Roslanders to bring Koro to help me." We had learned long ago, when we need help, that we could go into the water and do a slashing motion a certain way and make a sound in the water. This would get the attention of the Roslanders and they would come and help. One thing nice about the water, sound does carry a long way. Hopefully, they will hear it.

While we were waiting, Frank went up and got the cart and brought it down to the water's edge, and told me that he would give me a ride, back to the bay. We decided we would go ahead and start heading back to the bay. Hopefully, the Roslanders will show up shortly. The pain continued to get worse and my leg started to swell and all I could think of is I hope I don't lose my leg! I was really glad that we had packed everything up before we left to go swimming at least Frank didn't have to do it, by himself.

Frank picked me up and put me on the cart, there wasn't much room, but it'd has to do for now. I couldn't even stand on my leg. I tried to be brave and not scream out in pain. Frank would stop ever so often and asked me if I was okay as he looked at my leg, my leg continued to swell. This was not a good thing!

Then we heard yelling from the water and saw Tride, Trigut and Koro swimming towards the edge of the water. Frank pushed the cart all the way into the water, so Koro could look at my leg. Without missing a beat, she told me you got stung by a stingray, and it was a nice size one too. Koro needed to go get some salve to put on the wound; we needed to pull out the thorns that were in my leg, which is what is causing the swelling and the pain. Koro said she would also get me something for the pain. She told me to get into the water and let it soak my leg for a while. The warm water would help ease the pain too. Frank picked me up and carried me into the deeper water, I felt so silly, but there was nothing else I could do but let him.

Tride and Trigut stayed with us while Koro went to go get the salve. Trigut said, "Tridax had heard you call for help, and told us, we knew it had to be a problem, that's why we bought Koro. Frank told them "Thank you from the both of us." I wasn't in any condition to say anything.

It didn't take long for Koro to get back with salve and pain killer. Frank picked me up again and carried me to the edge of the water, where the cart was. He applied the salve to my leg, and wrapped it up. Koro had told him how to apply it and then to wrap my leg to make sure the salve does not get removed. It shouldn't take long for salve to pull out the thorns, but she will be in pain for little while. She handed the herb to Frank and told me this will relieve your pain. It will make you sleep for awhile; you won't be feeling anything soon. We thanked her for coming so quickly and helping me. She smiled and said "That's what I'm here for!" as she swam away.

Trido offered to go get the raft, and then they could pull me back to the bay. Frank said, "That's a good idea that would be great, thank you. I will go ahead and walk home with the cart. I'll meet you at the Bay tomorrow." I wasn't in any shape to argue with him. We just sat there on the beach waiting for Tride to return. Trigut stayed with us while Tride went to go get the raft and a couple merbeings to help him pull the raft. Trigut asked me, if I would like some energy healing, I told her Yes! As soon as she touches me, I could feel the heat and energy coming from her hands. Then the pain stopped, all I wanted to do is go to sleep.

All I can remember is lying in the cart, which was in the water still, having Trigut doing healing on me. I woke one time and saw Frank looking at me, he smiled and said hi, and then I was out again.

I woke up in my bed at the house; I had no idea what had happened. Then I heard Frank talking to me, it took a little bit to focus, but when I finally did, he was standing over me smiling again. I love his smile! I asked him what happened; he asked me "Do you remember being hit by the stingray?" I told him yes, and I remember waiting for the raft, but after that nothing. Frank reply, "Nothing like good herbs!"

I had so many questions; Frank finally stopped me and said, "Let me tell you what happened after you passed out." I told him, fine!

This is Frank's story: "While we were waiting for the raft, Trigut started doing energy healing on you, and the herbs Koro gave you, you were pretty much out of it. I was going to walk back with the cart, but after thinking about it, I decide to come back with you on the raft. Otherwise how would you get up to the house; after all you were pretty much out of it.

When Tride arrived back with the raft and his friends, I told him I was going to ride back too. He told me "I was wondering how we were going to get her up to the house." Frank told him, "Great minds think alike!" I put you in the raft, "Babe, you were really out of it! I had to push you over so I could get into the raft; you wanted the whole raft to yourself." Once we got back to the bay, you were dead to the world; I carried you up here to the house. You have been out for 18 hours.

I pulled the two thorns out and the swelling is gone. Welcome back, can you stand? I told Frank, I didn't know but I will try. I was a little unsteady on my feet, but the pain was gone. Thank goodness! I don't what to do that again!

Frank told me, we'll have to go back and get the cart later, and he also said the Clan leaders want to meet with us tomorrow morning. I asked him, did they tell you what it was about. He said "No, Trido said it was a good thing. I guess we'll find out tomorrow.

Frank asked if I was up for a walk, and I said sure, long as we go slowly, he agreed. We walked down to the bay, and we didn't see anyone for awhile, then Tridax and Trien came over to say hi. Tridax asked me how I was doing, and I told him fine. Little Trien wanted to know if I could play with her, so I did. We swam around and gathered shells and dived for them. Frank and Tridax joined us in a game of tag. It was another great day, no pain and got to play with the kids.

After awhile Tride and Trigut joined us, and then Koro, Trido, and Esaw all came over to see how I was doing. Koro wanted to check the wound; Frank told her the thorns had come out. Koro said, "That's great, you shouldn't have any more problems with it.

Trido and Esaw wanted to explain the protocol on what we should do when we go to the meeting tomorrow and what will be happening. Frank asked Trido, "Can you tell us what it is about?"

Trido said "No, all I can tell you it is a good thing." Esaw asked if we wanted to play cards, of course we said yes, so I went up to the house and got the cards. We played a couple of hands, but it was getting late, we said good night and we'll see you first thing in the morning.

40

WE WOKE UP early; it was a long night, wondering what was going to happen today. As we went to the waterfront, all of the clan leaders were there in the bay, by the center rock. We looked at each other, and went forward, did the side to side, head down acknowledgment, as Trido had instructed us to do yesterday.

Trido said "We have found something in the sea, but we don't know what to do about it. In the past you have talked about how you miss your family. We understand how sad that makes you feel. We also have talked about if you ever did leave us, you must keep our secret, and we can't have humans knowing where we are at. Agatha has been keeping journals, but also we need to keep our secret," Trido looked at me and said, "We would never take your journals away from you, Agatha, but we need to be sure that it will never be found."

Trido asked, "Do you swear never to tell anyone to the day you die, of our secret. We both said yes! Frank asked, "Has something changed, did you see a ship come by the island?" Trido said, "No, but we found a boat floating on the sea after the last storm. There was no one on it and it looks like it had broken away from somewhere. It does need some work; it looks like it has been out there for a while. But you can fix it Frank. It will take you some time but it is fixable, I think. After you have repaired it we could pull you out into the ocean, where other human would find you, if we need to."

Frank and I didn't know what to say or feel. I think we had lost hope of ever leaving here. We just assumed we would live out our life's here. All the clan leaders just looked at us, and were waiting for our reply. Then Frank said, "Yes, we want to go home, please let us have the boat. We would never tell anyone about you, we will never speak about the Roslanders, or any other Merbeings. As hard as it will be to not tell, we do understand why you don't want humans to know about you.

Trido said "The boat will be here tomorrow, we will push it to the water edge, so you can work on it." We thanked them, and left the meeting. We went back to the house at the tree line; we needed to be alone and to talk about what we needed to do.

As we sat by the fire, we started to get excited about going home. Seeing our kids and their families, what will they do when they hear we are alive? We knew the dinghy wouldn't have made it in the sea. But now we will have a boat.

The day passed by, we just started looking at all the wonderful things we had from the Roslanders. Also all the wonderful things we had found in the ancients cities and ship wrecks, we have been exploring the past few years. We were trying to figure out what we could take with us, and what we will have to leave behind. Of course, we will be taking my journals with us; there is too much information, to just leave it behind.

41

THE NEXT MORNING we got up, we could see a boat on the water. We walked over to it, it was about twenty feet long, it looked like a fishing boat, but not one from our time. Trido was right it would need a lot of work. It did float so that was a good thing. Frank climbed aboard the boat to look around on it, he said "There was a lot of junk on it and it must've been out to sea for a very long time."

After a little bit, Frank said, "Now it's time to get to work." We started by unloading the boat. Frank looked at the engine, but it was in pretty bad shape it was all rusted and the gas was bad. It didn't look like there was any other gas on the boat so the engine was pretty much useless for us. The Roslanders said "They could help us by cleaning underneath the boat". So they went to work and cleaned off all of the sea urchins, barnacles, one little octopus and whatever else was attached to the boat, it did take them a couple of days to get it cleaned off.

As we emptied the boat we found all kinds of things, it was like a time capsule, and it even had oars. It looked like people would find the boat, maybe use it and then the boat would take off again. Kind of similar to a ghost ship that just comes and goes! It took a couple of days just to get everything out of it before Frank would know what we would need to fix it up. He did decide that we could make a sailboat out of it. We still had our sails from the old ship and we had a lot of the wood that we pulled off it. We didn't want to burn the wood from the old boat, or any good wood we would find on the beach, so we had a good supply of wood. Just in case someday, we needed to build some kind of a boat. That day has arrived!

Once Frank made the assessment of what needs to be replaced or repaired, he made a too do list, in which order it needs to be done. After seeing the list, I knew it was going to take a lot of work, but we were up for the challenge. Because the boat was quite old, the floor was weak and needed to be removed and replaced. The good news was it was all wooden, so we could replace everything, which needed to be done, but the boat would still stay afloat. Happy Days!

We took the engine out; if we couldn't use it, then there was no point in wasting the space. Then we started removing the floor out of the boat, it was pretty rotten. The Roslanders had a sealer (tarft) for us to use, from our understanding, it was whale fat and some kind of plant they used, they use it in their underwater home.

We put tarft in between the bottom of the boat and the floor. The tarft was very unusual, it wasn't very sticky but when we put it on the wood it would hold fast. You could put it in layers once it dried, it was better than anything I have ever seen in my life. We also had to replace boards on the side of the boat. It wasn't the prettiest thing but hopefully, it will work when we are done. The next thing we had to do is install the mast, and the rigging. It wasn't easy but it was up and working by the end of the week. It's been three weeks and the boat is looking good. We're going to install some lines to the front so the Roslanders can pull the boat if need be. We're hoping the sails will do most of the work. The Roslanders had already told us they will lead us to where the humans would find us; we hope to be ready in a couple more weeks.

For the next couple of weeks we slowed down on our work because we didn't want to be exhausted when the time came to leave. We used some of the wiring on the boat to make a preventer. We didn't need any more accidents, and this would prevent the boom from accidentally gybing from one side to the other. We did have many parts from our old sail boat, but if we couldn't find something, the Roslanders would go down to the old ship and find the parts for us. The whole village was anxious to help us, I'm not really sure if it was to get rid of us or it was fun to do something different.

It was time for them to migrate back to their home under the water; they said they would be back in time to help us find our way home. Much of the work was done and all the parts removed from our old boat "The Big Dream", there wasn't anything else they could do to help us. There was a celebration of their migrating back to their home under the water. The celebration was great fun and a nice change for us, we have been working so hard on the boat the last few months, well it seems like months.

There was the normal Festival, the music and the dancing was fun. Frank and I usually dance on the jetty and the Roslanders would watch us. I felt like a celebrity because all eyes were on us when we first arrived and now our dancing is no big deal at the festival. They have festivals for every occasion, but none of them are as big as the "Batjak", that is a once a year event.

As the Roslander all swam off, it was sad to see them go, but we did have a lot of work to keep us busy. It's kind of like family, your glad to see them, but you're also glad to see them go.

The boat was shaping up pretty nice, it may not have all the bells and whistles of our old boat, but it is really looking good to us. Frank and I talked about what to name the new boat and we came up with "Homeward bound", it seemed appropriate.

Frank built some storage units on the boat to put our belongings into, to keep them from the weather. We weren't really sure how long we would be on the ocean and we needed some place to put our food and water. The Roslanders wouldn't really tell us how long it would take to get to a safe place, where we would be picked up. They did say be prepared to be on the ocean for a couple of days. It also would count on how the sails would work and if there was any wind. We really didn't expect the Roslanders to drag us across the ocean to safety.

Another storm was coming in so we secured the area and hoped it wouldn't destroy our boat. Frank said, "This will be a good test for the boat; if it can hold up in the storm then we will have a chance." If a storm came while we were out in the ocean, it would be good to know that it could at least withstand it. It was a pretty bad storm, if I had to rate it 1 to 5, and five being the worst, I would have to say it was a 3.5.

The first thing we did when we woke up, we looked out the window and there she was! We walked down to the boat to check it out; the good news was it was still afloat. We had to bail out the water and Frank found a couple leaks in his storage bins. A few parts came loose so we had to do a little bit more fixing up before we could continue to do the other repairs. Frank said, "It was really good that the storm came when it did. It helps us ensure that we would be safe on the ocean. It also made him feel much better about the boat, because it stood up to the storm".

We're almost done with all of the repairs and it's time to start loading the boat. We had pulled off the water tank from the old boat and installed them into this boat. So now we had the task of moving the fresh water from the woods to the boat. We smoked some fish, boar and chicken for the trip. We dried some sea plants and put them in containers that we had made or had them before. We decide to leave the statues and the other ancient artifacts that we found in the city behind, because they weren't ours to take anyway. We of course, are taking the gifts we received from the Roslanders. Also the gems, coins, and some other items we found on the sunken ship on the other side of the island.

All we had to do now is wait for the Roslanders to come back from their trip, which should be any day now. So we decide to kick back and relax and enjoy the island for a while. We started removing our house and putting things back where we found them, as much as we could. It was a hard thing to think that we were going to leave this place; it has been our home for so many years.

Roslanders started returning back from their migration. It was good to see Trido and his family. I think they were happy to see us too. All of Trido's family joined us by the boat, for dinner, they were surprised that we had gotten so far on the boat since they were gone.

We had to go before the Council again to let them know we were ready to leave and we would like their help. They agreed that five of the mermen, would help us out of the bay, and then on to the water where we would find safety. They told us to plan for three days, and bring many spears, in case there was any trouble. The water that we will have to cross is unknown to the merbeings. But is the shortest way to get us back home. They gave us a decoration; it was a kind of protection for our boat and our friends that will show us the way.

The council said "That they will miss us and they had learned much from us, and maybe not all humans are bad, maybe someday there will be peace once again between the humans and the Merbeings." Frank said "I truly hope so."

We finished putting the food and water on the boat and said our goodbyes at the festival they had done in our honor. Of course, it was wonderful to see everyone, just one more time before we left. There was music, and the children put on a show for us, doing flips, jumping out of the water, and dancing with other merbeings. Acrobats were amazing. At the end of the event, we went to sleep on our boat because we no longer had our home here.

CHAPTER

42

T HE NEXT DAY before the sun rose, the five mermen were there ready to go, also Trido and Esaw, and many of our friends. As the mermen pulled us through the opening in the Bay, I didn't realize how small the opening was. Trido had told us long ago that they closed the opening, so big ships couldn't get into the bay anymore.

The story I was told; many years ago a ship came into the bay and tried to trap their Merbeings; they threw their nets into the water and used explosives to chase Merbeing into the net. It was working until Trido and some of his friends cut the nets from the other side. Once they cut the large holes they called to the other Merbeings to escape through the openings. The Merbeings also pulled the ones that were injured and the ones that were killed out of the reach of the humans. This was to stop humans from having any proof that Merbeings existence.

As we cleared the jetty the Merbeings handed us the ropes they were using, and swam alongside us. As we set sail, the boat took off, we are making good time. The five mermen didn't have any problem keeping up with us. As we sailed along I thought about our old boat, how nice it was, and so comfortable. This boat wasn't even close, but it was the most wonderful boat we could ever have asked for.

We were told by the council that we needed to build a platform for the mermen's to sleep on at night. We used the bamboo from the forest and tied it all together, with the bigger bamboo to help make it float on the water. We had set it up into three different pieces and laid it on the stern. At night we could just roll it out and attach the three pieces together, the mermen would have a secure and safe place to sleep at night. The water was too deep for them to find a safe haven at night, and protect us from any predators.

The first day went without any problem, we saw whales and even saw some flying Mobula Ray, and they were huge. There were a lot of them, we would see three or four of them flying completely out of the water and then dive back without even a splash. They swam right under our boat, I told Frank I hope they don't jump into our boat. Frank replied "Well if they did, we would have dinner!" Night was coming and the mermen needed to stop for the night. It was too dangerous for them to travel at night in the open water. We put out their platform, it worked great. The mermen help connect it together and then went and caught dinner. We are settling in for the night, the merman took turns guarding, and making sure we didn't go off course. It didn't take Frank and I too long to fall asleep, one minute I was talking about how beautiful the star were, and the next I hear Frank snoring.

We woke up to the second day on the ocean; the first thing we noticed was three of the mermen were gone. The other two told us, they went hunting and will be back soon. We went ahead and pulled up the platform back on the boat and pulled the anchor up. Just as we completed getting the platform secure, the other three mermen, showed up with breakfast. We ate our breakfast and the merman told us we had to keep a sharp lookout for sharks in this area. This is the part of the ocean where the monster sharks rule.

As we set up our sails, we noticed that the mermen were staying closer to our boat, before they just swam in front of us, or just hung around us. Frank said "I guess they mean business."

We were on high alert, when it happened.

We were sailing along when all of a sudden the mermen gave their warning to each other and we knew what it meant, there was danger. Frank and I looked around trying to see what was going on, but there was nothing to see. Then all of a sudden we were hit on the bow, it knocked me off my feet. Frank was at the helm, trying to see what it was. The mermen all moved to the starboard side, and it looked as if they were just waiting for something, for another attack!

Frank climbed up on the bow to see what was going on when all of a sudden we were hit again and this time Frank went flying into the water. I ran to the side of the boat to see if he was okay, and he was shaking his head trying to figure out what had happened. Then I looked up and I saw it, the monster shark that the mermen had warned us about. It was coming straight at Frank; I yelled SHARK! I could see we were moving away from Frank, I dropped the sails, so Frank could get back on the boat. The shark was coming too fast, and then all of a sudden the five mermen were there in between the shark and Frank. Two of them were waist high with the spears ready to be thrown and the other two were up on their tails, with their spears out high. I couldn't see the fifth one, and then all of a sudden the mermen attacked. The fifth one was underneath the shark; he came up and shoved the spear into his throat area. The two that were waist high shoved their spears into the sharks face and the other two went high and shoved them into the upper part of his head.

The shark pulled away, and Frank climbed on the boat just in time. The merbeings went into tactical mode for the second run on the shark. This time Frank was ready, he grabbed the spears and threw them at the mermen, they caught the spears and they were ready for action. As the shark turned around and started coming towards us again, you could tell he was mad, he was going faster than before and looked like he meant business, and he still had the five spears in him. This time the mermen set up with two on each side of the shark and the fifth merman was between us and the shark, he was doing a little dance, trying to get the shark to come at him. As he got close the four mermen attacked again this time they shoved the spears in even farther and as the shark was getting prepared to ram our boat the fifth merman dived and Frank shoved his spear in between the shark's eyes. I guess that's all it took, it was over as fast as it started, and the shark just disappeared.

Frank yelled, "Let's get the hell out of here, and no one argued the point with him. The mermen took the lead as usual; they kept a watchful eye out for any more sharks. The wind was with us so we started making good time, but as we looked out into the ocean we spotted a few more sharks, these were much smaller and the mermen didn't really act like they cared about them. Later I asked them, why weren't you worried about the other sharks? They said "They were going after the free food, so we didn't have to worry about them." I just said, Oh!

It was starting to get dark, we decide to stop again. We set up the platform for the mermen for the night; a couple of them went fishing and brought back more fish, and sea plants to eat. I told Frank and the mermen that I would take the first watch, and they didn't even argue with me about it. I was told to make sure the boat kept going towards a certain star, they all pointed at the star. I know how to steer the boat, I figure I would be fine.

They all settled in for the night, as I kept the watch out for any danger. I really wouldn't know what to do if something happened, I guess just scream. It was a hard day for the guys, I figured at least I could do is watch out for while.

CHAPTER

 **43** 

I WOKE UP THE next morning next to Frank; I had gotten Frank up for his shift, before I lay down for the night. I guess the mermen were keeping an eye out this morning. We did our chores, brought in the platform, made breakfast and talked about our plan for the day. One of the merman told us, "We should see something today; a couple of us will go ahead of you to see if we can find anything, when we get closer." The wind was light, so we were not moving very fast, but there wasn't much we could do about it.

About midday the mermen decided they would go out on their own to see if they could find any humans. Two stayed behind and the other three went out looking for some humans. They were gone for about two hours, when one of them swam up to the boat and said "They had found some more humans, but they were in a raft like the one we had. They told us that the other two were pushing the raft towards us, the humans looked alive, but they weren't in very good shape. They look like two big humans and one small human."

We headed the boat towards the direction they were leading us; it didn't take long to run into the other mermen. They brought the raft alongside of the boat and we could see there were a couple and their child in the raft. The couple looked to be in their thirties, the little boy looked about six. They didn't look too good; I went on the raft to check them out. They were all still alive, but they definitely needed water and food. I helped the child and the woman get on board and Frank came over and helped with the man. We gave them water to help with the dehydration, and after a while the man became conscious and he thanked us for saving them. But also wanted to know who in the hell we were, as he looked around the boat. Then he passed out again. I can only imagine what he was thinking.

After a little while he was conscious again, this time he introduced himself. I'm Gary and this is my wife Larie and our little boy Joel. We asked them what happened to them. Gary told us that they were out on their yacht fishing, when all of a sudden they were attacked by pirates. There were six of them and we didn't have a chance, they were on us before we knew it. They asked us for our money and jewelry and gave us a choice of dying now or later, and we chose later. They told us to get on the raft and have a nice life. That was last time we saw the yacht.

Gary said "He wasn't sure how long they would last; we figure we weren't that far from land, but the current pulled us farther away from land. It was a good thing we had water and food in the raft, there is no way we could have lasted as long as we did otherwise. He thanked us again, and said he wasn't sure how it happened. One minute we were going one direction, and the next thing I knew we were here with you." Of course, we knew how they came to us, it was our mermen friends!

Frank told them that we have been marooned on an island for five years and we are trying to make it back home. We have been out on the ocean for 2 1/2 days now and were still looking for landfall. It was getting dark, and we really didn't want to spend another night on the ocean, but there wasn't much we could do. We told Gary, Larie and Joel to go ahead and get some rest, and we'll wake them if anything happens.

We had them sleep in front of the boat, on our bed. This would give us the opportunity to talk with the mermen and see what was going on. Frank went to the end of the boat and leaned over and signaled to the merman it was safe to come out. He asked the mermen could they hear any ships, and they said "Yes there are many boats out there, but they are not coming towards us." They did tell us that we were going in the right direction. We were surprised to see Joel looking at the mermen and then he just waved at them, and the mermen waved back. He wanted to know why the men were in the water, and we just told him they were helping us get back home. He just said ok, then we told Joel to go back to sleep and everything was okay. He went to his parents and crawled into bed with them.

As the evening closed we were getting ready to settle in for the night, and we were trying to figure out how our mermen could get some rest. They told us the water wasn't so deep, they had found a place to stay for the night. They would be safe; we didn't have to worry about putting out the platform tonight. They also told us, they would be leaving us soon, there will be too many humans around, and that we would be safe now. Just keep heading this direction and you will see land soon. But they will stay until the humans show up, but will stay out of site of the other humans on the boat. We understood, and thanked them, and wished them a safe trip home.

As we settle in, Frank asked me, "Doesn't Gary look familiar to you?" I told him yes, but I wasn't sure from where. Then it hit me, it is the guy from the picture in the chest, we found last year. Frank smiled and told me "You're right! I guess we'll have to give him back his chest." Then I pointed out to Frank, it doesn't make any sense. We found the chest over a year ago, and now he's back on the ocean and has lost his boat again! Frank said "Let's just wait and see what he has to say after we have been rescued." I agreed with him and settled in to wait and see if we do get rescue.

Then we saw a light on the water and it looked like it was coming towards us, we thought maybe it was search ship or a helicopter, we started getting excited and then the light disappeared, it must of turned away from us. We didn't think we could do anything about it, but Gary was awake and stated that he had a flare gun in his raft. Frank jumped into the raft and grabbed it, and took aim and shot it in the direction of the light. As the flare started to dim the helicopter turned around and started coming towards us, it had seen the flare. It didn't take them long to reach us, as the helicopter hovered above us they hollered at us that there would be a ship within an hour. That was the longest hour of our life since we lost our first boat.

As we waited to be rescued, we could see the mermen in the distance; they waved at us and understood we couldn't respond back. We wanted to tell them thank you so very much for saving us again, but we couldn't do it, without Gary and his family seeing them.

Gary and Larie turned to us, and Gary said "Here's my business card, please come see us when you get settled in." We agreed we would call them, when we had gotten things settled.

CHAPTER

44

WHEN THE RESCUE ship arrived, we helped Gary's family get aboard and told the ship captain that we would follow them in our boat, because we were not willing to give up our boat. We had too many wonderful things we wanted to keep. He agreed, mostly because we were not the people he was looking for, they were looking for Gary's family. It took another couple hours before we arrived on land and then we had to wait to be processed. I guess being gone for five years raises some flags for the government.

Once we got cleared by the Coast Guard, we called our son Frank Jr., to let him know that we were alive. Frank tried to convince him that it was really us, and it took a little while to convince him, but we finally did. Frank told him the story that only Frank and his son knew about, and I still don't know the story! Frank Jr. agreed to call his sisters, Twila and Maria and let them know what was going on. Frank Jr. started asking his dad all kinds of questions. Frank finally stopped him and said we'll tell you everything when we get home. Frank Jr. asked to talk to me, I got on the phone and when I heard his voice I started to cry, it was so wonderful to hear his voice. I just couldn't talk; Frank took the phone away from me and told Frank Jr. "We'll call back later after we get a room. Frank Jr. said, "He'll get his sisters to come over to the house, so we can all talk together tonight. Frank said "Great, we'll talk to you soon son!" Frank had tears in his eyes too.

We were in Florida and we needed to get to Houston, Texas, we didn't want to take the boat so we rented a car. We put "Homeward Bound" into a storage unit, until we could get things settled. Frank also wanted a friend of his to look at boat, because he felt it was a very old boat, just by the craftsmanship and the way the original frame was done.

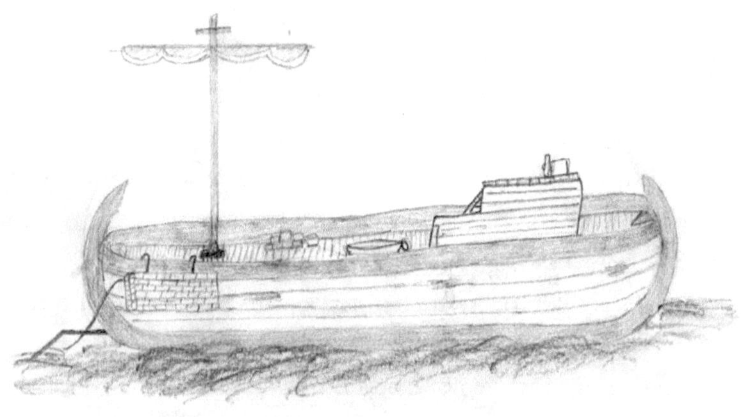

It took a little while but we did get processed through the governments' paperwork, we loaded up the car with all of the wonderful things we brought with us. It was going to be a long drive, but there was no way we were going to fly, the car was fast enough, after only walking for five years everything seemed so fast.

Before we headed off to Houston, we had dinner with Gary, Larie and Joel; we took the chest along, and left it in the car. We told them we had found a chest we think belong to Gary. But we had found it over a year ago and couldn't understand how that could happen. Gary and Larie just sat there with their mouth open. Then Gary said he had been in a storm and had lost his first boat in it. Lucky he wasn't too far from land and was rescued by the Coast Guard. It was the weirdest storm, it was clear one minute and the next, my boat was going every which way. After talking a little more we found out it was the same storm that put us on Rosland.

Frank excused himself and when out to the car, and when he came back he had the wooden chest. Gary and Larie couldn't believe their eyes. Larie started to cry, and she told us that she had given the chest to him on their first anniversary. It was supposed to be a good luck charm, and it was as far as I'm concern. He didn't die in the storm.

Frank handed the chest to Gary; all they could do is thank us. I told them sorry we drank the cognac and used the cards. But everything else is still there. Frank told them, "We planned on trying to find you when we got rescued, but we figured the odds were against us. But here we are! We enjoyed the rest of the evening and said our good-byes. We will be heading to Houston tomorrow; it will be wonderful to see our kids.

On our trip to Houston we talked about how we would explain our adventures, about the people that we lived with. We both agreed that we would call them island people (natives), this way we could talk about our new found friends without giving away what they really were. It was weird seeing city after city and people everywhere.

The welcome home party was wonderful; it was just our three kids and their kids. They said "They didn't want to overwhelm us with all our friends and other family members, at this time." That was fine with us. We spent the next month getting to know everybody again. In the last five years, both our daughters had gotten married, and both had two children now. Frank Jr. was still married to the same wonderful woman he was when we left and he had added another boy to his family. We missed so much; they have all grown up and have wonderful children. It was so hard because we couldn't tell them the truth about the wonderful Beings we had become friends/family with.

The following weekend we had all of our friends and the rest of the family join us in a crab fest. It was nice to see everyone; our friends had gotten fatter and really looked old. They couldn't believe how great we looked, we both were slim and tan. All the swimming didn't hurt our muscle tone either. There was a lot of laughter and plans to be made to see each other again. Cleaning up the crab fest was a lot harder here, and then the one we had with the Roslander Clan. I think everyone would have thought I was crazy if I just flip the table into the water to clean it off.

We stayed with Frank Jr. family; he had a little cabin on his property that we could use. It was nice to spend time with the grandsons; Daniel and Douglas, Daniel looked like his dad, and Douglas looked like his mom. They were so different; we did a lot of fishing and hiking with them. We even learn how to play video games. Not that we were any good at it, but it was just fun spending time with the grandsons. Tridax would have had fun with them.

We had already told our kids that we were going to buy another sail boat, a schooner if we could find one we liked. The plan was to live on the schooner, and travel around the islands again. Needless to say all of the children were very upset with us, but we told the kids, we needed to live our lives. We did promise them that we would not be gone more than two weeks at a time, and we would call every other day. They are worse than my parents were!

The insurance money came in for our boat "The Big Dream" so we went down and bought a schooner, we had our eye on it for quite a while now. With all the other money we saved in the last five years, we could pay the schooner off. That was a great feeling. We still had the artifacts and jewels we had found while we were on the island. We didn't what to use them if we didn't have to, we were afraid of the problems it could cause for us. It's just nice to know we have them, for now!

The kids and their families all joined us in getting the schooner loaded up and double checking all of the equipment. They were making sure that we were going to be safe. They brought us an emergency radio just in case something happened. We had to break the schooner in; all of us went out and enjoyed the bay for the day. The kids had a great time in the water; we did a little fishing and enjoyed our family. It was great to be back with them. But it was time for us to get back on the open ocean; we really missed the freedom of the water.

CHAPTER

E WERE BOTH so excited to be heading out into the ocean again. The kids gave us a great sendoff and now it was time to see if we could find our friends again. In the last few months we have been looking over different maps, trying to figure out where the island could be. We thought we had a good idea where they were located, but we were wrong.

The idea was if it took us three days to get to Florida, it shouldn't take us that long to get back to the island in our new schooner which we named "The Dreamboat 2".

I have been rewriting my journals, since Frank and I have been back. Everything was in shorthand, so I have rewritten them into long hand. I wanted to make sure nothing was missed or incorrect in my journals, before I let anyone read them. I also have added things that Frank and I would remember as I rewrote the journals.

One thing about sailing; there is a lot of time to write at night, it reminds me of the time we spent on the island. All you hear is the ocean, and the calls of the sea life around you. We learn so much from the merbeings, and enjoyed the ways of the island.

You were never in a hurry or too busy just to enjoy the day. We still do this; I think it drives our kid's nuts sometimes.

As we sit out in the ocean, there is no land to be seen, every once in a while we think we see one of the merbeings, but once we get closer they are not there. They did tell us, we would never see them again.

Maria, our daughter and her husband, James had joined us a couple of times. She's always asking to read my journals but I tell her "Not now, the time will come when you can." I want to clean up the journals before anyone can see them. She understood but didn't look too happy about it. Maria and James, and their kids Treva and Enola, would bring their boat out, and join us for a couple of days. I think they just wanted to keep an eye on us.

Twila, Dennis and our granddaughters Tina and Sharlene also came out and joined us. Sometimes Sharlene would stay with us for a week at a time. Tina was older and had better things to do then hang out with her grandparents.

In the summer; Sharlene and Tina would stay for a couple of weeks. We had a great time with them and got to know them both better. Sharlene is young enough to believe in mermaids (Merbeings). I tell them stories about the island and the Merbeings, without them knowing they are true stories.

Tina on the other hand asked a lot of questions, but I think she believes that they are real. It was always nice spending time with the kids and our grandkids. But we did enjoy our time alone on the water. Frank Jr., Wanda and the boys, couldn't come out as much as they would like, but we did see them a lot when we were on land.

We have been back in Texas for awhile now, but we still enjoy going out on our boat, and we go out as often as we can. When we do, the kids watch the weather for us, and if there are any storms in the area, they call us on our boat and tell us to come on in, most the time we listen to them, but sometimes we don't!

All of the grandchildren came out with us this time; we had a great time with them. At night we told them stories about living on the island. They did enjoy Grandpa and Grandma's stories about our adventures on the island and all the things we discovered while we were there. They are still young enough it doesn't hurt to talk about the merbeings; they think we are just making it up. Our granddaughter Sharlene is the one that listens to every word and details about the merbeings.

Tina asked us about the dream rooms, and the places we visited. She wanted to know when we were going to go to Utah, and to see the redwoods in California, we had told them about. Frank and I looked at each other, and we said why not.

This is when our oldest grandson Daniel asked, "Why don't Grandpa and you go visit it for real, you promised each other you would!" Of course, Tina our oldest granddaughter had to join in and asked, "Why don't we all go?"

Then Frank said "Let's make it a family trip, get a couple of RV's and see the sites of the United States. All the grandkids started cheering. I settled them all down and said we need to talk to your parents first. We don't know if they can take the time off.

For the rest of their visit, that is all the kids could talk about. Frank pulled out the maps we had of the United States, and was showing the kids, where we would be going. I just smiled and told him, you're going to have to talk to our kids. He smiled back and said, "How can they tell us no, we have been missing for five years.

When we arrived back at the dock, our kids were waiting for us. Frank looked at me and said, "No time, like the present to talk to them." I had to agree; because I knew the kids wouldn't keep it a secret for long.

We asked our kids to come on board; we had something we wanted to talk to them about. First thing that came out of Twila mouth was your not taking off are you? Well kind of, come on in and we'll tell you about our great idea.

Clan Members:

Roslanders

Trido – Father of Tride, Clan Chief and King of Utopia
Esaw – Mother of Tride, Partner of Trido, and Queen of Utopia
Tride – Son of Trido and Esaw
Trigut – Partner of Tride
Tridax – Son of Tride and Trigut, Grandson of Trido and Esaw
Trien – Daughter of Tride and Trigut, Grandson of Trido and Esaw
Rostri – Partner of Jaros, of the Jamicaer Clan
Rosder – Master Stone cutter
Istin – Ancient one
Koro – Healer

Frank and Agatha clan

Frank Jr. and Wanda – Daniel and Douglas
Twila and Dennis – Tina and Sharlene
Maria and James – Enola and Treva

Jill – Aggie friend from the senior home and writing the prologues.

Don't miss Jolynn Rose's next novel

More Adventure with Agatha and Frank

Available soon!

Turn the page for an excerpt.....

NOTE: This journal was written before we published
the Roslanders books. Jill (Aggies's friend and publisher)

PROLOGUE

After we spent five and half year being stranded on Rosland Island, where we were kind of rescued by the natives of Rosland, we called them the Roslanders. We had been living with the Roslanders, while we were on the island. The natives had found a boat that we used to leave the island, and helped us get to where other humans would find us. The time on the island was wonderful; the Roslanders took us into their clan, and taught us how to survive on the island. It was hard to leave the island, and the Roslanders. I think if it wasn't for our children and grandchildren we would of never came back.

I kept a journal of our time there, but it is time to make new memories with our family. I hope you enjoy our new adventures and maybe even learn a little history as we go along. Remember, I am a history teacher after all!

Aggie

CHAPTER

1

WE HAVE BEEN back for five years and we have settled into the day to day life. We go out sailing as much as we can. Our kids join us whenever they can. They do have their own lives. We do enjoy it when we get the grandkids all to ourselves. With that said, we had all the grandkids for a week, there are six of them. All wonderful and they enjoy listening to Grandpa and Grandma's Stories of our island adventures. We were talking about going into the dream room and how much we enjoyed going back to our family trips, when we were young. The dream room is a place we found on Rosland Island. It was an ancient city, which had been covered up by the vegetation.

Anyway, this is when our oldest grandson Daniel asked, "Why don't Grandpa and you go visit those places for real? You promised each other you would!" Of course, Tina our oldest granddaughter had to join in and asked, "Why don't we all go?" The next thing we know all of the grandkids are cheering and agreeing with her. Grandpa wasn't any help, he agreed with them too.

Then Frank said "Let's make it a family trip, get a couple of RV's and see the site's of the United States. All the grandkids started cheering. I settled them all down and said we need to talk to your parents first. We don't know if they can take the time off. I thought to myself, there is no way I'm taking six kids across the country by myself.

For the rest of their visit, that is all the grandkids could talk about. Frank pulled out the maps we had of the United States, and was showing the kids, where we would be going. I just smiled and told him, you're going to have to talk to our kids. He smiled back and said, "How can they tell us no, we have been missing for five years. Funny, how Frank always uses that card, when he wants our kids to do something for us. I just smiled at him.